(S)mothering Bernadette

ALSO BY DANIELLE GRAINGER

THE DENTON HEIGHTS SERIES
Under Her Wing (Book 1):
The Shasti and Madison Story

In Her Cage (Book 2):
The Jaleesa and Tina Story

Within Her Grasp (Book 3):
The Marta and Shanice Story

By Her Command (Book 4)
The Rowena and Minjung Story

THE BERNADETTE SERIES
Wrecking Bernadette (Book One)

(S)mothering Bernadette (Book Two)

Becoming Bernadette (Book Three)

Desiring Bernadette (Book Four)

Loving Bernadette (Book Five)

(S)MOTHERING
Bernadette

BOOK TWO IN THE BERNADETTE SERIES

DANIELLE GRAINGER

Paperback ISBN   978-1-953734-15-0

First Edition 2021

9 8 7 6 5 4 3 2 1

Cover design by Sarah (Forcoverservice)

Published by:
Bibi Books Publishing Company, LLC

Dedication

This work is dedicated to those who recognize and stand up against abuse,
no matter what form it comes in.

Acknowledgments

Big thanks go out to those who have helped me learn about this lifestyle. Thanks especially to Miss A, Miss S, Miss M, and GBoo. I also want to thank the wonderful and amazing people in the Kik group who answered my many questions and helped me with my understanding. I enjoyed being a part of your lives and appreciate the connections I made with you.

Table of Contents

Chapter 1
Dumped

She dumped me. Dumped me before we had a chance to get started. I won't say that I'm wallowing in my apartment on a Friday night, but that's precisely what I'm doing with a wine glass in one hand and a Twix cookie bar in the other. One week ago tonight, I drove from Cincinnati to Columbus for my first and what turned out to be my last, monumental weekend with Mistress Ciara. It was amazing. She was amazing. I licked a lot of pussy that weekend. She spanked me and chained me up. She knew how to push my boundaries, boundaries I didn't know I had. But I guess we won't have a chance to explore those boundaries anymore because of, you know, the whole she-dumped-me thing.

"Dumped is a strong word," I say to my quiet living room. "Fine," I answer myself, "Tossed out? Thrown to the curb?" I pause for a moment. "Used?"

Used. I mused on the word for a long time. Did she *use* me? Yes. But didn't I *use* her a little bit, too? Was it just a long weekend of uninhibited, unabashed sex? For both of us? All of us? How can I forget that Nik and Mommy Tatiana were there, too? It was an orgy. Just sex. Wham bams, thank you, Ma'ams, and that was it.

So why does my heart hurt so badly?

"Because you wanted her to fall in love with you," I say out loud. The naysayer in me answers, "There was no chance you were ever going to be Mistress Ciara's submissive longer than that one weekend." Why would anyone want a soft butch thirty-something nerd as a sub?

I look at the keyboard on my laptop. I originally sat down at my desk to surf the web, to take my mind off her. But now she's the only thing I can think of. I bet I, Dr. Bernadette Garneau, professor of mathematics, is *not* on her

1

mind at all. Or anyone's.

Ahh, but do I really want to be someone's submissive? I mean, really? I take a sip of wine and put the glass down carefully on the coaster. It's one of those lighthouse coasters Jen and I got when we went to Bar Harbor that first summer we were together. She moved in with me right after that trip. She's probably wondering where that coaster is now. I can't help grinning as if I got away with something. Why did I take it when I moved out, anyway? Spite. For sure. A stupid thing, really. She and I had dissolved long before I even knew what was happening.

"*You* broke up with *her*, genius," I say out loud. Maybe I was trying to grab some power back. "And so that's why she's still living in *your* house on your five acres, and you're here in a third-floor walkup."

I growl at myself in an attempt to shut down the perpetual thought wheel. How Jen was able to come up with the money to pay November's and December's rents, along with the late fees for each, was unbelievable. She got the money in less than a day. I thought for sure I'd have grounds to evict her and get my house back. She must have borrowed money from Cassidy, the twinkie I now know she'd been having an affair with while we were still together, although I can't prove it.

"Grrr," I growl again and gulp some wine. Why sip when gulping gets the job done faster?

I take a deep breath and wonder what I want. Do I really want to be someone's submissive? To give someone power over me? Control over me? How much control? Mistress Ciara and I didn't talk too much about control. She just took it. I used safewords, and she honored them. That was good. But that was just for sex. I liked it, but I think maybe I want to give up control in more ways than that. I want someone to tell me what to do, but not in a mean, bossy way. I want someone to make all the decisions. I mean, I think I do. But not in a fifty's housewife kind of way. Although lots of people dig that. No, I want to work and have my career.

"Gah, I have to get off this hamster wheel." I sigh and click open *Kinks.com,* the website that got me into this mess in the first place. And as I've done every day since I got back from Columbus, I click on Mistress Ciara's page. Does she have a new submissive? Did she say anything about our life-altering weekend? And the answer to both of those questions is no.

Every single day, her page has been the same. It's as if it didn't happen. As if *I* didn't happen.

But it did happen. And I have the bruises to prove it. I mean, they're fading now, but I earned them when she bent me over the kitchen table and slammed her BBC into me, the Big Black Cock dildo I would come to both love and hate. My bruises commemorate that first intense orgasm that weekend.

I moan at the memory, close the website, and power down my laptop. There's no sense torturing myself anymore today. There's always tomorrow.

I turn off the lights in the living room and head for bed. There's no one but me in that bed. But that's okay. I have my tablet to keep me company. Lisa, my friend on *Kinks.com*, turned me on to lesbian BDSM stories. I had no idea stuff like that even existed, but now my tablet is filling up fast with stories I download from, like, everywhere. I even follow a few authors now and get notifications when they come out with new stories. I think they call themselves writers of erotica, but whatever. It floats my boat, and that's all I care about.

After washing up and brushing my teeth, I hunker down in the bed and pull up an e-book I've been reading by E.J. Dubois. I wonder if that's her real name or if it's a stage name. No, it's not called a stage name. I can't remember what it's called, but if that's her real name, then she's courageous, unlike me. No one knows I have a kinky bent. No one knows I am submissive and looking for – well, at least I think I'm looking for – a female dominant as a 24/7 life partner. Or am I just looking for a Domme in the bedroom?

Stop.

No hamster wheels. There's no time for that. I'm keeping E.J. Dubois and her story waiting. I settle into my pillows and click on my e-reader app. And there it is, *The Transformation of Five*. I find my electronic bookmark and glance at the curtains. Yep, they're still closed tightly. And my lights are off, so no one can see what I'm about to do. Ahh, what is Sarah, AKA Five, up to now?

Sarah's heart beat faster when she heard the first guests arrive. Her desire to please her Ma'am far outweighed her comfort. For the first time ever, she was to be the drink cart at one of Ma'am's private parties. Ma'am's other girls were envious of her, of course. That had been clear all afternoon, but they'd have their turns soon enough. Ma'am had a lot of parties.

Sarah was grateful that Ma'am allowed drink carts to wear knee pads. She didn't know what was worse, the grinding of her knees on the hardwood floors or the carpet burns. She was well-versed in both because Ma'am sometimes made them stay down on hands and knees all day as a punishment, head down, kissing Ma'am's feet whenever she got near. It was an honor, a gift even, to be able to touch Ma'am in any way. The orgasm she'd given Ma'am in the kitchen that morning with only her tongue was an absolute privilege and one she would never take for granted. Afterward, Ma'am inserted a finger in Sarah's vagina to make sure the experience had aroused her. Ma'am worked hard at conditioning her slaves to become aroused when servicing others. "Good, good, girl," she said when her finger came out covered with Sarah's slick arousal. She gripped Sarah's chin and said, "I believe you are truly ready, Five." Sarah swooned with dizziness at the praise.

Ma'am always said she was firm with her girls but not cruel. Some of the other Dommes shook their heads at Sarah's Ma'am, saying she was too soft on her slaves. Sarah would have to disagree because she'd had other Owners who were mean just to be mean. Ma'am was always fair. For example, Ma'am flogged, spanked, or caned her girls practically every day to remind them of their place. She called them maintenance floggings. Her five girls had gotten a flogging that very afternoon, in fact, as reminders of their roles. Sarah wore the welts on her back proudly, but she was disappointed that the cooler strapped to her back covered them.

Sarah wasn't sure what types of bottles she carried but knew they would be the most expensive sodas, waters, beers, wines, and ciders money could buy. Ma'am spared no expense for her guests. The other girls' jobs were to make sure Sarah's cooler was kept well stocked. Well, except for the trash girl. She also had to crawl around the party on her hands and knees with a box for trash on her back. Trash girls got abused at Ma'am's parties. Pinched and slapped until they bruised. Bare ass cheeks reddened all evening long. Words like whore, fuck meat, and worthless trash were written on their bare skin with Sharpies that took weeks to wear off because Ma'am would never let the trash girls scrub away the words. Sarah was scheduled to be the trash girl at the next party. It was every girl's rite of passage, she'd been told. She couldn't wait.

A cool hand caressed her bare buttocks. "Five," Ma'am said quietly to Sarah, "get a move on." Sarah was the last girl that Ma'am had acquired of the five, and Ma'am always called them by their assigned number, never by name. Sarah had only been with Ma'am for two and a half months but knew that eventually, she would come to think of herself as Five, not Sarah. Just like One and Two. They never mentioned having any other names before those. It was like they couldn't remember.

Ma'am liked her girls to be silent most of the time, even more so at parties, so Sarah didn't acknowledge her verbally. She simply started moving. Ma'am's guests knew about the silence-is-golden rule, but sometimes they'd go out of their way to make one of Ma'am's girls cry out in pain or ecstasy, but they'd rarely succeed.

5

Ma'am's girls were well-trained.

Sarah made her way toward two guests who had seated themselves on the couch. The load on her back was heavy, and yet it was oddly comforting to know she was of good service to her Ma'am. Crawling made her heavy breasts sway like cow udders back and forth beneath her. She was keenly aware that her sex was open and displayed for all to see. She centered herself in front of the women, keeping her head lowered and her knees spread so they could use her body if they wanted to.

"Oh, what a darling human drink cart," one of the women gushed. She had a slight English accent. Sarah couldn't see her and preferred it that way. She was an object, and objects didn't see or have opinions. She felt bottles lifted from her back and heard the unmistakable sound of caps being removed.

"Oh, right here," a second woman said, and then Sarah heard the caps land in the glass jar strapped to the cooler. This woman sounded older. She petted Sarah's head and moaned her approval. "Chin up, dear." Sarah lifted her chin but stared straight ahead and did not make eye contact. The woman gently ran the back of her hand over Sarah's cheek. "Beautiful, isn't she?"

"Mm hmm," the English woman said. A hand ran over Sarah's hip. "Such a lovely young and firm body." Sarah decided to think of this one as the Dame.

"Tongue out, dear," the older woman commanded. Sarah obliged and pushed it out as far as she could without seeming grotesque. "Oh, yes. I may avail myself of that tongue later."

The Dame chuckled and asked, "Would you like that, girl?" Sarah moved her tongue as if licking, which caused the older woman to laugh.

"Ahh, I see why your new owner kept you on. You're adorable. You can put your tongue back in, dear."

The Dame's hand that had been stroking her hip moved underneath to Sarah's belly. "Hard as a rock," she said. Her hand moved upward and found one of Sarah's breasts made long and full by gravity. Two fingers latched onto the hardened nipple and gently squeezed. "Hard nipples, too. Beautiful little pebbles."

Sarah felt a gush of wetness soak her pussy. She wasn't sure if it was from the praise or the women touching her body. Probably both. Another pair of hands reached underneath from the other side.

"Damn," the older woman said with a rough tone. "Nice firm titties." She slapped one of Sarah's breasts, but Sarah didn't flinch. Titty slapping was one of the favorite past times of Ma'am's guests, so it was expected. The woman slapped her again. "Nice." She slapped Sarah's breast three more times but then stopped. Sarah was disappointed. The slaps weren't hard enough to leave bruises. She wanted a trophy from the evening. Not to worry, the night was young.

"Feel her ass, Bobbie," the Dame said to the rough-voiced titty-slapper.

A pair of calloused hands, obviously no stranger to manual labor, groped her ass cheeks. "Nice. Very nice.

Mmm. When do the strap-ons come out?"

"At the top of the hour," the older woman said. "You know she always makes us wait."

"I'm gonna make this one squeal. I'm gonna slide my dick inside her pussy until it bottoms out. And those drinks on her back are going to break from the pounding I'm going to give her. And after that, she's going to break."

The Dame scoffed. "Oh, Bobbie, you always say that. These slaves are well-trained. You know that. She works them every day. They are not going to cry out."

"Bet?"

"The usual?" The Dame said.

"Sure," Bobbie said. "One hundred dollars says I will make this drink cart cry out when I fuck her this evening. And that's any time I fuck her tonight," Bobbie sneered. "I plan on staying hard the whole night."

"Bobbie, you are delightfully nasty," the Dame said with glee in her voice.

Unbeknownst to the two bantering women, Sarah's breathing had gotten labored. She wished Bobbie would take her right then. She could feel her wetness sliding down her inner thighs already. She couldn't wait for the top of the hour to transform into a fuck cart.

"Oh, my God," I say out loud. "I want to be a fuck cart, too." I reach under the covers to find that I am as wet as Sarah. I touch my slick folds and rake the moisture up to my clit. I circle my clit a few times and know I am going to blow quickly. Thank God I have no Mistress, Domme, Goddess, Ma'am, Owner, or Dame to tell me what to do anymore. I can touch myself and orgasm whenever I want.

I reach over and pull out my spare dildo from the bedside cupboard. No lube is needed tonight. I rub the bulbous head over my growing clit. I could cum from just this. No, I like penetration. I rub the dildo through my swollen arousal and then slowly ease it inside. Wait, no. Just the head. I pull back out, but not all the way. Just enough to make me want it more desperately. In again. Out. Just a few inches each time. As I'm micro-thrusting, I reach down with my other hand and circle my clit again. Ahh, that familiar stirring. I spread my knees wide, like Sarah in the story. Although I'm lying flat on my back in my bed, I imagine I'm on my knees, presenting my sex to Bobbie and her strap-on.

The strap-on suddenly fills me to my depths. She pushes it in hard against my cervix. It hurts just enough to make me buck my hips. "Fuck me," I whisper to the imaginary Bobbie. Sarah can't talk, but I can. "You got it, little fuck cart," Bobbie says, grabbing my hips for leverage. The strap-on pulls out and then plunges into my depths over and over and over, smashing my cervix with every thrust, raking over my G-spot again and again.

Sarah can't cry out, but I can and do when my core slingshots my release, and my orgasm roars through my body. I moan as pulse after pulse grips me deep inside my womb. "Ahhhhhhh," I say over and over as the strap-on doesn't stop plunging inside me. Finally, the pulses slow, and the strap-on stops, then slides out of its own accord. I am a figurative puddle lying in a literal puddle of arousal and release. Hopefully, the three towels underneath me have served their purpose. I close my eyes, and it takes several long minutes to catch my breath.

I could never be a silent fuck cart. I'd get punished a lot, wouldn't I? My inner walls clench at the thought.

Ahh, but there's no Domme in my life to punish me, now is there? Mistress Ciara dumped me, remember? Fine. I don't need her. I'll just find someone firm but fair like Sarah's Ma'am, and then I will finally live happily ever after.

Chapter 2
DIY

I wake up at the usual time, but it's not a workday. I toss and turn for a while, hoping to get some extra sleep, but it's futile. The hamster wheel has begun. I wasn't good enough for Mistress Ciara, and I'm probably not good enough for anyone. Who would want me? I'm too old and not a cutesy fem. My bad haircut doesn't help either, but I don't know how to fix that. I do like the color, though. Someone called it natural wheat blonde once. Ahh, but who cares? No one will see me today. Except that's not true, I have to get food. And wine. You can't ever forget the wine.

After a quick shower to freshen up, I don't bother to dress. I love the feeling of being vulnerably naked. I was nude from the first minute I stepped into Mistress Ciara's home, except when she let me wear a tight and revealing bra and boi shorts when I was cleaning her townhouse, which I honestly didn't mind doing. I liked helping her and thinking that she might be pleased with me. She wasn't pleased enough, I guess.

I turn up the thermostat on the way to the kitchen because Cincinnati is cold in December. Oh, and the whole naked as a jaybird thing makes you kind of cold, too. I get the coffee pot going and stare at it to make it go faster. That never works, but I try. I lean both forearms on the countertop and then take a few steps back so that I'm bent at the hips. I keep my legs straight and stretch my hamstrings. Ahh, that feels good. Maybe I need to get more exercise. I move my feet apart and open myself up. My breasts hang down and sway like Sarah's did in that story. A wave of arousal spikes through me. But there is no Domme behind me with a strap-on. A week ago, I was bent over Mistress Ciara's kitchen table like this, my private parts in the air, open and available. That was, of course, after I'd already licked and sucked her pussy to orgasm within minutes of arriving. After that, she bent me over her table. She and her

BBC had their way with me.

"Mmm," I moan as delicious arousal swirls through me again. I'd been at her house for probably less than an hour when she brought me to the best orgasm I'd ever had. Up to that point, that is. Of course, the very next day, I passed out from an even more incredible release. She'd bound me with chains, and I'm not talking figuratively. She had eyebolts in her living room furniture and kitchen baseboards. I know I wasn't the first person chained there for anyone to use. And use they did. All of them. All at once. Nik and Mommy Tatiana and Mistress Ciara. They filled all my holes at the same time. My pussy clenches at the memory. I could cum right now, but I don't. There's coffee to be had.

I open my eyes and stand up. I brighten when I see that my ancient coffee pot has finally finished brewing my magic morning elixir. My mood sours again when I remember the boundaries Mistress Ciara pushed. I groan. No, I will not think about that stupid part of my visit.

I snag a coffee cake from the box and head to my desk in the living room. I power on my laptop and, as usual, hit up Mistress Ciara's page on *Kinks*. Nope, not a single thing has changed since last night. As I drink my coffee, I toy with the idea of sending her a message. Lisa has forbidden me to do so, though. Lisa is not a Domme or anything, but she's much more experienced with BDSM and matters pertaining to Dominance and submission. She says that Mistress Ciara made it very clear that I was not to contact her again. Lisa also said I have to think of that weekend as a weekend orgy, and that's it. It's over and done with. "Move on," she told me emphatically yesterday in a *Kinks* message. I should message her back. Later. I'm not in the mood to get scolded again. I'm doing enough of that on my own.

"Well, either way, Mistress Ciara is over and done. And that's fine," I say with much more conviction than I feel. I slam down my coffee cup for emphasis. "Dammit!" The coffee spills all over my walnut desk. I grab some tissues and sop up what I can before it ruins the surface. "Whatever! If I can't contact Mistress Ciara, then I'm going to update my profile and hope she sees it and cries because she had me once upon a time and stupidly let me go." I laugh, knowing how ridiculous this statement is. She hasn't given me or my profile a thought since I left. Not even once, I'm sure of it.

I open my profile page and spend several long minutes rewriting my image. Now it reads that I am an eager-to-please sub up for anything and ready to learn. Well, anything within my hard limits, that is. Satisfied, I hit the repost button and sit back, waiting for the Dommes to pour in.

I carefully unwrap the coffee cake from its cellophane wrapper and devour it in two bites. I obviously need another and zip to the kitchen for round two of cake and coffee. It's too early to go to Kroger, I'm not quite awake enough to deal with people, but hey, it's never too early to watch porn, right? How shall I imbibe? My favorite porn star, Betlinde? No, I like watching her at night so I can dream about her owning me afterward. Porn sites online? Meh. Nothing interests me there right now. The girl-on-girl scenes aren't realistic to me. I mean, I know nothing in porn is real, but I'm beginning to wonder if anything is real.

I take a sip of coffee and say out loud, "What do you want, Bernadette?" After a moment, I conclude that I have no fucking idea what I want.

When in doubt, I read one of Lisa's stories. She calls herself Rachels_toy on *Kinks*. Rachel is her Domme *and* her wife, which positively fascinates me. I would love to have that kind of relationship. Jen was nowhere near that for me. Thank God we didn't get married during our four years together.

"Gahhhhh!" I groan out loud. Why does Jen keep showing up in my brain? "I dumped your ass! Except I'll never be truly rid of you until I get you out of my house once and for all." I bow my head, slam my eyes shut, and place my hands together in prayer. "Please, oh, please, Lord, let Jen default on next month's payment. Let January start a very happy new year for me."

Nope, nope, nope. No more thinking about exes. I blow out an annoyed breath. Muriel and her antics await me on *Kinks*. I am just about to click on Lisa's page when I notice a red number one hanging innocently off the mail icon.

"Oh, joy. Probably more dick action." I shake my head and mutter, "Let's see what this guy wants to do to me." When I first joined *Kinks*, I was appalled at the horny guy messages I'd regularly get in my mailbox, but now I decide to be amused by them.

I click on the mailbox, and my eyes get wide. This is no guy. It's a message from someone named Goddess Julie. I'm frozen. Do I dare open it? What if it's, like, a real Domme? Like Lisa's wife? Or, or, or what if it's some poser Domme that Mistress Ciara warned me about?

"You'll never know unless you click it, moron," I say, hoping no one ever hears me talking to myself this way.

I click on Goddess Julie's message.

GODDESS JULIE: Hello, gorgeous.

Okay, that was short and possibly even sweet, but that's it, nothing else. I laugh. There is nothing on my *Kinks* page that would indicate that I am gorgeous. I only have a naked boobs shot. Okay, it's a pretty good boobs shot; my nipples were perky and tight in the picture, but that's the only picture of me I have on my page. Oh, I posted some flower pics and a sunset shot in the Colorado mountains. That's all. So, for this Julie person to tell me I'm gorgeous is positively ridiculous because I am not. So, I should hang up right now, delete her message, and forget about her. I was on my way to read one of Lisa's stories, anyway. Muriel has certainly gotten herself into new trouble, and I must find out what it is.

But the hand controlling the mouse doesn't move for some reason. Okay, okay, I'll admit it. I'm curious. Maybe it won't hurt to look at her page and see her pictures and profile. My hand agrees, and I'm on Goddess Julie's page within seconds. She is an attractive blonde-haired twenty-something woman wearing a cream-colored corset and not much else. Well, she's wearing a lot of makeup, and the crop in her hand looks ready to spring into action at a moment's notice.

I read her profile, and she claims to be a fair yet strict Domme. Slaves will be treated with kindness but disciplined appropriately, she declares on her page. Slaves will understand that Goddess Julie's needs will be first and foremost in their minds and actions. Nowhere do I see evidence of her being a Fin-Domme, a financial Domme, a Domme for hire. But she could spring that on me at any time. Should I make that a hard limit? "I will not, nor ever intend to, finance your petty wants and greedy needs." I snort out loud. Oh, that would get the Dommes lining up.

"Slave," I mutter with a sneer. "I don't want to be anyone's slave. Even Mistress Ciara said I was not slave material." I don't know what brought her to that conclusion because I was pretty much her slave that entire weekend, but I must have lacked some fundamental slave *thing*. "Whatever," I say with a dismissive hand wave. "I'm not your slave anymore, Mistress Ciara, so who cares what you think. Buh-bye."

I get back to the task at hand and find several more delightful pictures of Goddess Julie. She seems uber-proud of her breasts and with good reason. They are firm and full, and each one seems like a nice handful. I squirm in my seat. I'm getting turned on by her photos. Before I can stop myself, I reopen the mail message and type a message back.

CRYSTAL_TOY: Hello

Nothing binding. Nothing revealing. Just ponging back her ping. If she wants to pursue, I'll be listening. But I won't be waiting. For some reason, I'm no longer in the mood to read and leap up from my chair after powering down my laptop. I have to get dressed. There's shopping to do.

I dictate my shopping list into the notes feature on my phone as I drive the couple miles to the hardware store, but not the local mom-and-pop place. They kind of know me there. When I still lived in my house, I'd frequent that place all the time. No, I'm going to DIY Supplies, the big box home improvement store. Do you know how those detectives on TV can tell if you're buying ingredients like fertilizer to make bombs? Well, I've got a kinky list of supplies that only someone in the lifestyle would recognize.

Clothespins. Where does one find clothespins? Ahh, laundry aisle. Derrr. I spot them, and a rush of heat flushes through me. My nipples harden. The pins are made of wood and come in packs of a hundred. That's a lot, but what are you going to do? My hands are shaking when I pick up the package. Lisa told me that clothespins are a regular part of their intimate moments. I imagine my nipples clipped and then my inner thighs, labia, earlobes, lips, nostrils, eyebrows. The sweet sensation of arousal causes my breath to labor. OMG, I'm getting turned on in the hardware store. She said I'd have to work up to putting one directly on my clit. My pussy clenches at the thought.

I grab some laundry detergent, which I don't need, but I want it for my cover story. I head down the aisle but come to a full stop when I see the rope. It's a twenty-five-foot package of white nylon clothesline. With rope, I can bind myself to the chair or the bed. I can pull on it and spread myself wide open, spread eagle. Of course, I have to make sure I have a good knife or hefty pair of scissors handy if I can't undo the knots. Oh, God, could you imagine? Uh, hello, 911? I've tied myself to a chair and can't move. Of course, how I'd manage using the phone is beyond me in this scenario, but I laugh and put the clothesline in the cart. Wait, should I go with chains instead? Nah, it would be too hard to explain why I have chains in my cart, mainly because I live in an apartment.

In the corner of the store is a small pet supply section. I had the foresight to measure my neck before I left. Could you imagine me trying on collars right there in the store? There would be no hiding the kinky college professor in aisle thirty-seven. Yeesh. I run my finger over the various collars. Definitely nothing pink or girly. I want something weighty that I can feel. Ooh, here's one like Mistress Ciara put on me. My heart sinks as I rub my thumb along the leather. Someone else is probably wearing my collar right now. She's probably got someone else chained up on her living room floor. Nik is lubing up his strap-on. Mommy Tatiana is cooing in the sub's ear.

A sob catches in my throat, and I swallow hard to choke it down. No, no, no. It was just a two-night orgy. It's over and done with I will not give Miss Ciara the satisfaction of crying in public. Absolutely not. I grab the collar and find a matching leather leash to go with it. Should I buy dog food so no one will know what I'm up to? No, that's just dumb. Buying kink supplies at the hardware stores is dumb, too. Whatever. Ooh, look, bandanas. I can use them as wrist and ankle cuffs. Or a blindfold. I grab a pack of ten. I won't need ten. Wait, maybe I will. I might want to gag myself, too. Ahh, perfect.

I check my list to make sure I have everything. Yep, all systems go. On the way to the checkout, I see an aisle ender with earplugs. Earplugs for sensory deprivation. Yes, yes, yes. I throw the pack of twenty in the cart.

I try not to notice the overwhelming Christmas lights displays. I used to love Christmas. I mean, I still do, but Jen was never into it. She grumbled and complained every time I asked for help putting lights on the house or getting the tree and decorations out of the attic. That fourth and final Christmas we were together, I didn't put lights on the house and only pulled out a couple of things. I had to have my mom's ceramic NOEL candle holders and her reindeer cardholder. I found a few of the snow people figurines my mom had collected throughout her lifetime before she passed and set those up, too. Mom never allowed us to call them snow*men*. Good for you, Mom, a feminist in her own right.

I get in the long line at the checkout, hoping no one looks too carefully at what I am buying. I don't see any nosy bodies and let my mind wander philosophically. Am I a feminist? I always thought so, but how can I want someone to own me? How can I want someone to take charge of me and tell me what to do? Is that counter to feminist thinking? Can you be someone's submissive and also be an independent woman? Ahh, this is so confusing.

I move up a few feet in the line. I was almost, but not quite close enough to put my purchases on the oversized belt. Belt? Dang it, I forgot to get a belt. I need it for self-flagellation. I groan and roll my eyes. I got a taste of BDSM and power exchange, and it's taken me over. I never knew that a person could be this horny all the time. Wait! The leash. I can use that. Now, that's serendipity.

As I move up and put my kinky DIY supplies on the belt, I decide that I am, indeed, a feminist. The most basic tenet of feminism is that women have the absolute right to choose their own paths and sexual proclivities, partners, and activities. I have voluntarily entered into this lifestyle of my own free will. There. The matter is settled.

Stashing my new purchases in the trunk, I head to Kroger for the usual. Frozen pizzas, frozen dinners, Coca-Cola, wine, coffee cakes in the box, and cookies. Should I get potato chips? Ha! That was a rhetorical question if I ever heard one. I should probably get milk and cereal and eggs or something, but I can't be bothered. That's bordering on healthy. After checking out, I head to the car.

I'm just about to lift open the hatchback when I hear my name.

"Hi, Professor Garneau."

I freeze, paralyzed. When I finally thaw, a young woman with jeans and a pink ski jacket stands behind a cart heading toward Kroger. She smiles at me. She has a familiar face and is probably one of my current or former students. "Hey," I say, "how are you?" I'm embarrassed that I don't know the young woman's name.

"I'm good," the young woman says. "I'm almost finished with that last problem set. There are a couple of hard ones on it."

"Oh, yes, of course." I still have no idea which course or section she's in. "I have to challenge you, get you ready. Final exams are next week."

"Don't I know it," the young woman groans. "I think I'll be ready. Oh, hey, will you be teaching Calculus Two in the spring semester?"

Ahh, she's one of my Calculus One students. "We don't know our schedules yet, but probably not. I usually teach Calc One and Elementary Functions."

"That's too bad," she says with a frown. "You're such a great teacher."

"Oh, thanks. That's sweet of you to say." My face grows warm.

"Well, it's true. I guess I got lucky this semester." An awkward silence follows until she says, "Well, I should go." She lifts her hand and waves even though we're only a few feet apart.

I also wave and say, "Have a good one. See you in class."

"Yep. Bye."

As soon as the young woman is out of earshot, I exhale nervously and cautiously lift the rear door. Thank God it wasn't open when she walked by. She'd know what a kinky kinkster her professor is. I know everything I bought is in dark bags, but still. My heart sinks again. What am I doing? Why did I buy all this kinky stuff? Who am I?

I put my groceries in the trunk and pull up at the Hungry Hamlet's drive-thru. I buy two separate meals. One for now and one to reheat later for dinner. I also buy two cherry pies for dessert and an ice cream cone, which I obviously have to devour on the way home.

Two trips up the three-story walkup with my packages, and I shut and lock the front door to keep the world out. The ice cream and lunch I ate in the car driving home have cheered me up immensely, and I whistle as I put things away. The kink stuff gets shoved in the dark recesses of my closet. I will deal with it later when I am braver.

I click on the computer to see if Goddess Julie has responded. My eyes widen when I see the red number one on my mailbox. I click it, and sure enough, Goddess Julie has answered. Oh, God, this could go in a million different directions.

I take a deep breath and deliberately keep my clothes on.

Chapter 3

Goddess Julie

I stare at her message for several long minutes without seeing the words. Am I ready for this? Do I really want this? So soon? What is *this* anyway?

"Well, Bernadette," I say out loud, "there's only one way to find out." I briefly think about pouring a glass of wine but change my mind. I want a clear head this go around.

I read Goddess Julie's return message.

> GODDESS JULIE: crystal_toy has needs, doesn't she? Desires that only a Goddess can fulfill. But you do realize, hun, that it's not about you and never will be? It's about me. Always. It's about how you can serve me and take care of my needs. Being Goddess Julie's slave will be fulfillment enough for you.
>
> You've looked through all of my pictures, haven't you? I know you have, down to the last erect nipple. Subs always do. But are you capable of sacrificing your own comfort and needs for mine? Oh, I don't think you're a mindless, worthless twat, btw. Slaves are a precious commodity. But finding the right slave to suit me can be, well, challenging. Do you think you might fit? Are you special enough? I'm not sure. I need convincing.
>
> Tell me how I can use your body to satisfy my needs, crystal_toy. Tell me how I can use you, all of you. Why

would I, a Goddess, want anything to do with you? Tell me.

A sweet pulse of arousal travels to my southland. A glance at the closed curtains and the locked front door, and I am ready to tell this Goddess how she can use me. I stand up and shed my clothes, not caring where they land. This makes me feel more submissive. I click the *respond* button and start typing.

> CRYSTAL_TOY: The first thing Goddess Julie could do is put a collar around her sub's neck, with a matching leash, of course. Probably something red to match Goddess's lovely corset. The collar sends the message that Goddess is in charge and calls the shots. Perhaps next, she will strap her sub down on a bed with legs spread as wide as possible, allowing easy access to her sub's body to do anything she wants.
>
> Perhaps Goddess wants to climb on top and have her pussy licked by an eager tongue. Her sub's soft lips will attach firmly to Goddess's clit and suck her to orgasm. Goddess will cum all over her sub's face as her sub excitedly laps up every last drop of her nectar.
>
> Or perhaps Goddess will want to see how much pain her sub can take. Clips on nipples. A spanking over her lap. A flogger. A cane. A wooden spoon.

I throw in the wooden spoon idea to show her that I have a sense of humor and that I'm not all about getting laid. I grimace when I realize that I kind of *am* all about getting laid. And that is pitiful. I scoff. That's where my life is right now? Really? Getting laid? And by a stranger on the internet? Oh. My. God.

I stand up, leaving Goddess Julie's reply unfinished, and find myself in the kitchen pouring that glass of white zinfandel I said I wasn't going to have.

The other five bottles are chilling in the fridge, patiently waiting their turns. I grab a chocolate cupcake pack out of the pantry and then head to the bedroom to fish out my new clothespins. Once back at my desk, I take a sip of zin and try one of the clothespins on my index finger. It kind of hurts. I can't imagine clamping one of these things on my clit. Or my nipples, but I'm going to try.

The mere thought makes my nipples hard. I place a clothespin over my erect right nipple and close it down gently over the tender skin. I take it off before it's all the way closed because it hurts so much. How the heck do people stand this? Another sip of zin gives me courage, and I try again. I cry out as the pain shoots from my clamped nipple directly to my pussy. This is nothing like those stupid chip clips Mistress Ciara had me use. Those were child's play. This shit right here is serious. The pain pulses, and I try to relax and bask in it. I breathe through the waves until I can't take anymore and pull it off. I don't think I will ever get used to that much pain. Maybe I'm not a pain whore like Mistress Ciara said I was. Mmm, but I did like her spankings. Well, sort of. They hurt. They really did, but because I trusted her, I allowed myself to relax into it. Maybe that's what I have to do with the clothespins. Relax enough to *enjoy* the pain. But not now. I'm too chicken.

I devour the chocolatey goodness of the first cupcake while deciding what else to say to this stranger who calls herself a Goddess. After another sip of zin, I conclude that zin isn't necessarily a good match for cupcakes. And I also conclude that I am not going to make the same mistakes I made with Mistress Ciara.

In my response, I purposely don't use the word slave. Maybe she'll take the subtle hint that I am *not* anyone's slave, even if I act like one. I also don't use that pesky upper/lowercase syntax because that shit is annoying. Now, where was I? Oh, yes. Time to add in some hard limits and then wrap it up.

CRYSTAL_TOY: This sub vehemently dislikes CNC and needles and breaking of skin of any kind. This sub is not into golden showers or scat play. This sub does not want to be shared with men. This sub does not enjoy public humiliation or public sex play, either.

So, this sub wonders what types of things inflame Goddess Julie's desires? What makes Goddess Julie feel powerful? What makes Goddess Julie wet and desiring of a sub's attention?

This sub would love for Goddess Julie to tell her, but only if it pleases the Goddess to do so.

I lean back and reread my unintentionally long message. I realize that I never used the word I or me. I referred to myself in the third person. A psychologist would have a field day with that. But I can't worry about it right now and hit the send button.

I lean back and close my eyes. Ahh, what are the chances this is a real Domme? And that she's *the one*?

"Slim to none," says my annoying skeptic.

I'm going to be much more careful with this one. No pictures. No visits, even if she lives in the apartment downstairs.

I pick up one of the discarded clothespins and press it open and closed repeatedly. With the fingertips of my left hand, I gently tease my right nipple until it hardens. It's such a subtle sensation, but it travels straight south. My hips move slightly, almost on their own. I have a lovely rhythm going, and I am enjoying the high. Feeling brave, I pinch the skin around my nipple and offer it up as a sacrifice to the clothespin. The pain pulses where the clip closes around the flesh. It travels directly to my clit and my entire pussy. I spread my legs but don't touch. I want to feel the pain. I tease my left nipple, so it's even harder. Sweet pleasure on the left combined with salty pain on the right, and I am in ecstasy. It isn't long before the second clothespin pinches down.

I pull out the drawer containing my quickly growing collection of dildos. I reach for the purple monster. This thing is thick. I bought it because I want to feel filled as it slides in and out. I pull out a black bag and set out three anal plugs alongside three anal dildoes, all of varying sizes. Lube will be essential if I decide to use any of these today. They scare me, though, and I haven't tried any of them yet. Maybe I'll get brave and try a double penetration later. Maybe.

But first, the purple monster. I lick the head of the monster and then slide it in my mouth and suck on it a little. I thrust it in and out with tiny motions, never getting anywhere near the back of my throat. My legs, unbeknownst to me, have spread themselves wide. It must be time, then. It's funny how my body always knows. I bring the dildo down to my opening and press the head against my nether lips. This wets it further, and I bring it up and over my clit. My arm accidentally knocks against one of the clothespins, and pain shoots through me, but it is a weird, contradictory pain. I twist the other clip and am rewarded with more arousing pain. I rub the monstrous dildo up and over my clit several more times getting her ready for the fun times ahead.

I am just about to slide the dildo inside when I see the mailbox icon light up. No way. She's back already? Sure enough, it's a message from Goddess Julie. I click it open and decide something bold before reading it. If Goddess Julie is like Mistress Ciara, she will take away my orgasms and my right to touch myself, so I'm going to fuck myself with this dildo while I read her reply. I insert the head and moan as it stretches my walls. Mistress Ciara's BBC was as big as my purple monster. Maybe I should call mine the BPC. Ha, Big Purple Cock. Oh, it feels delectable as it slides in. I pull it out and slide it back in a little further. Soon, the pistoning dildo has me breathing hard. At one point, it bounces against my cervix, and I stop all motion in order to enjoy the sensation. I press on the suction cup end to make sure the dildo is good and lodged inside me. Next, I open her message.

GODDESS JULIE: Are you touching yourself, slave? Sliding your fingers through your pussy? Coating them with your arousal?

Short and to the point. I stand up from my chair and squeeze my legs together, so I don't lose the monster lodged in between them. I pull a sturdy acrylic clipboard out of the bottom desk drawer and put it on my chair. I carefully lower myself so the suction cup end of the dildo adheres to the clipboard. I stand tentatively, and sure enough, the suction cup is holding. Eureka, it works. I lower myself a little and feel the monster move further inside me. This is fantastic. Hands-free fucking.

I lift and lower myself on the monster as I answer Goddess Julie back.

CRYSTAL_TOY: Yes.

One word. This is my only response. Within a second, she replies.

GODDESS JULIE: Good. I like an aroused sub. Tell me how you're touching yourself, crystal_toy. Are you unclothed as every slave should be? Are your nipples clipped? Are you using both hands? Or a toy? Is there a dildo sliding in and out of that gaping wet maw between your legs? An anal plug, or better yet, a horsetail held inside your ass? A leash in my hand guiding you to play with yourself in front of me? Let me hear you cum loud and proud, crystal_toy.

I thought she would tell me *not* to touch myself, that only she could authorize it, but she did the opposite, and her words ignite me. I increase the pace and flick the clothespins. I moan with desire. But then I slow my pace so I can answer her.

CRYSTAL_TOY: Yes, Goddess Julie, I am nude. I like the way it makes me feel. Reading your post made my legs open. I'm sporting clothespins on my nipples. They bite just right. I am currently riding a thick dildo. Its massiveness is sliding in and out of my pussy. Are you watching, Goddess Julie?

She replies immediately. She wants me to slow down the pace of the dildo and then stop altogether. She wants me to sit impaled on the monster inside me. She then instructs me to slowly unlatch one of the clothespins and breathe in as the blood recirculates there. Then the other. It is exquisite, and I tell her so. Next, she tells me to sit comfortably and attach a clothespin to my inner thigh. She wants to know how it feels, and I am truthful when I say it hurts good. One by one, she has me attach clothespins to both inner thighs and then move up until I have reached my swollen pussy lips. She tells me to

23

go slow and put one on my fleshy outer lips. I feel so dirty doing this. The clothespin becomes covered with my arousal and keeps slipping off the mark. One time, it twists, and the sharp pain smacks me hard. That pain was different, I tell her. That pain wasn't nice. She says she understands but to try again, and I do successfully. I feel its grip, but it doesn't really hurt. It just adds to the sensations. She instructs me to put a clothespin on the other side. It goes on more easily. I feel so many different places of sensation that I don't know where to concentrate my focus.

GODDESS JULIE: Breathe in the pain, crystal_toy. Feel the pulse points of every single clothespin attached to your skin. I want four more pins to go on. Two pins on each nipple. Do it, please. After that, slowly rise off your silicone lover and bounce down an inch or two over the head. Feel the head at your entrance. This is the head of my dick waiting to plunge into you. I press against the pins, making you feel the pain as your breasts bounce with each of my thrusts. Cum so I can feel your walls squeeze my hard dick. I'll release my cum inside you, the cum I've been saving up all week for you, crystal_toy.

I feel the pain points like so many little heartbeats all at once. I fasten the pins on my nipples, two on each nip this time. I feel so heady, and I tell her so. I stand up off the monster dildo and then bounce up and down on the head as instructed. I feel like she's teasing me with her dick when she knows I want it deep inside. But she won't let me have it. I pull out, and the dildo falls to rest against several of the pins attached to my labia. I breathe in at the jolt of pain. Who knew it could feel like this? I am positively dripping wet. The slickness oozes down my thighs, coating the clothespins. She tells me to flick the pins on my legs, then my pussy, and lastly, my nipples. I tell her I am dying. She says I am surely not.

GODDESS JULIE: I need my dick inside your pussy, crystal_toy. Do it. Let me pound you. Feel those pins move as I use your body. Feel that orgasm build. Squeeze

24

my dick with your spasms, crystal_toy.

I plunge down on the dildo, and the clothespins flap as she promised. The sensations over my whole body are incredible. I rock my hips up and down, twerking the dildo in and out. This feels so good that I wouldn't be able to stop if she commanded me to. An orgasm begins deep inside, coiling up like a fist. I ride the fist until I can't any longer. Shock waves unleash through the clothespins straight to my pussy and back again. I continue to fuck myself on the dildo as I shriek my release. All too soon, the waves slow and then finally stop. It's always disappointing when that happens, but the pain points are still pulsing. She asks me how I feel, and I tell her that she is still hard inside me, that the pins moved exquisitely, and that the pain still pulses. She instructs me to take the pins off slowly. She emphasizes the word slowly, and I understand why. Each pin is its own pleasure point. I tell her how exquisite I feel and how high I am flying.

> GODDESS JULIE: I like fucking you, crystal_toy. Your cum bathed my Goddess stick in proper tribute. I also came. Did you know that? I shot my cum deep deep inside your womb. I left my Goddess seed embedded there. You are part of me now, crystal_toy. In fact, I require you to change your name on *Kinks*. Change it to GoddessJuliesSlave. Let everyone know that my seed is growing in your womb. That soon, your only life's goal will be to please and pleasure me.

I pluck the last of the pins off my body and bask in the flight of afterglow. I am so high right now, high on sex and endorphins and Goddess Julie. I tell her I don't know how to change my name on *Kinks*. She says it's up to me to figure that out, or she will be displeased. She says that I won't like it when she is displeased.

She sends another message. She wants me to change my profile picture, too. My eyes open wide as I read what she wants. My high diminishes. She tells me to post a public picture for all to see of me kneeling in the nude with the words, "Goddess Julie's seed is inside me," written on my belly in black Sharpie marker. I tell her I need a selfie stick. She tells me to go shopping. I'm disappointed because I didn't want to go out again.

She says she has to leave and that I have until midnight to get my name changed and my picture posted. I agree to go to the store, but I make no move to get up. I can't because I'm still flying around the room high on endorphins. She signs off, and I close my eyes. I doze in my chair, the dildo still lodged firmly inside me.

Chapter 4
Noticed, Needed, Nurtured

It's already dark by the time I get back home. The selfie stick has been purchased, and I've taken a few practice shots. It wasn't that hard to figure out, but it's not in my nature to take pictures of myself. I mean, I take the occasional picture if I'm on vacation, which I text to my brother and Dad back home in California, but that doesn't happen often.

I pull my new Sharpie markers from the bag. What does she want me to write again? I log back into *Kinks* and click on our message thread. I copy down her words on a post-it note, "Goddess Julie's seed is inside me." I look down at my belly and realize I'm going to have to write this upside down. No worries, it's just a different orientation, an elementary geometry problem, a 180-degree rotation.

I plan out the position of each word in my mind and start to write. It's incredible how well a Sharpie marker writes on skin. This isn't toxic, is it? I write the words *Goddess* and *Julie's* on my skin, but I hesitate before writing the word *seed.*

I calmly recap the marker, place it carefully on my desk, and sit back. I stare at the closed curtains. "What am I doing?" I say slowly. What does this even mean? Her *seed*? At first, I took it as a sign of her possessing me, owning me. But now it just sounds weird.

I close the message thread with Goddess Julie and open the one I have with Lisa.

CRYSTAL_TOY: Lisa? I need advice. Whenever you get a chance. I don't want to bother you, but it's about matters of the heart. I met someone. Can you check her out for me?

I hit the send button, knowing she probably won't see it tonight. And I need to get this thing done by midnight or else. Or else, what? I have no idea.

My phone vibrates from the other end of the selfie stick. It's Lisa. Darn, I wanted to do this through messaging, not voice to voice.

"Hey, friend," I say into the phone.

"Who'd you meet?" There is an excited lilt to her voice. "In person or on *Kinks*?"

"*Kinks*," I answer succinctly.

"Who? I'm sitting in front of my computer; my cursor is blinking in the search bar."

"Goddess Julie."

"Got it." I hear keys clacking from her end. "How'd you meet her? *When* did you meet her? And have you had sex yet?"

"She messaged me. This afternoon. And yes."

"What? You met her this afternoon, and you've already had sex? That was fast. Too fast. Well, o-kay." She drags out the syllables as if trying to wrap her head around the whole thing. "Let me just check her – whoa, Bernadette, she is hot! OMG."

"I know, I –"

"Nope, hang on. Let me get through all the pics." Lisa makes tiny clucking noises as she clicks through Goddess Julie's pictures. "No wonder you had sex with her right away. I'm a little turned on right now."

"Well, you are a sucker for a good pair of boobs," I say with a laugh.

"Ah, yes. I am a boob girl." She laughs, and it puts me at ease a little bit. "Let me read her profile."

"Okay." I feel very exposed as I sit there nude. I pull the phone out of the selfie stick and get up to put on a sweatshirt and a pair of sweatpants. I was getting kind of cold anyway.

"She's into discipline and says she's firm yet fair. She seems kind of young, though."

"Yeah, younger than me."

"That's okay. Plenty of Dommes are younger than their subs. It's not about age; it's about attitude. And there are a lot more subs around than dominants, so we have to take what we can get, right?"

"I guess," I say, but as I say it, I realize that I don't want to settle. "So, what do you think? Should I …"

"Get into a relationship with her?" she cuts me off. "Hell no, B. Not yet."

I smile. For some reason, she's started calling me B. I guess Bernadette is a mouthful. "Because?"

"C'mon. You barely know this woman. Not long enough to get into a committed relationship."

I am silent on my end. I mean, I know she's right, but I was flying pretty high this afternoon. And I liked it.

"B, you still there?"

"Yeah."

"You can't," Lisa says emphatically. "Not yet. Promise me you won't."

"Okay. I won't."

"I know you want to, but you have no clue who this person is. I assume your, err, liaison was done through messaging?"

"Mm hmm." And now I feel like an idiot. Lisa now knows what kind of a pervert I am. Getting off with a stranger on a Saturday afternoon. What is wrong with me?

"Hey, hey, hey, B. It's okay. You're fine. It happens."

"*What* happens?"

The laughter that follows my innocent question is soothing and southern accented, and it makes me smile. "Oh, B. One-night stands with a stranger. Or, in your case, one-afternoon stands. But, look, this doesn't have to mean you marry this person. I know you want to belong to someone; you absolutely have that right. You're trying to find *the one*."

"Yeah, I thought Mistress –"

"Mistress Ciara was *not* the one, B. She just made you feel things you'd never felt before. There is no way you could sustain four-way orgies like the one you had with her."

"I wanted to try." I make my voice sound pitiful but then chuckle so she knows I'm not serious. Or am I?

"When you find that perfect top or Domme or whatever, then you'll truly feel fulfilled in all kinds of ways. Not just an afternoon or weekend of sex. Mistress Ciara was *not* the one, and this Goddess Julie is not the one either. Can I ask you a question?"

"Of course."

"Did she demand tribute of any kind? Money? Getting things on her wish list?"

"No-ooo," I singsong.

"What kind of tribute, B? And before you answer, I have to tell you that I don't like this."

I hesitate for a moment and then spill everything, including the words written on my belly, which I didn't finish, and the selfie, which I didn't take. I don't tell her that I premeditatively went out and purchased the selfie stick and the markers for the explicit purpose of doing Goddess Julie's bidding. I don't want to confirm Lisa's suspicions that I am a total idiot.

"B, you can't commit to someone, anyone, after one online session. And the fact that she asked you to means she is not the kind of dominant you want looking after you. She sounds selfish or, in the least, self-centered."

"Is there a difference?"

"Absolutely. Selfish people care only about themselves, and if it hurts you, they don't give a shit as long as they get theirs. Self-centered people care about themselves first generally, but they do care if it hurts other people."

"I guess you can't be both then, can you?"

"You can, but in different situations. This Goddess Fuktard needs to get a clue. She's young and has to learn, but not at my friend B's expense. Not on my watch."

I chuckle at the newly assigned nickname. "Umm, so what do I do now, Lisa?" I lay my phone down flat on my desk and wrap my arms around my body. I am so screwed.

"Okay, listen up. If you ever thought of me as your friend, then you will take my advice. Do not engage with Goddess Julie again."

"But ... "

I can't finish the sentence.

"But what?"

"I don't want to be rude to her." I know it sounds dumb, but I have always been polite to people. I don't want Goddess Julie to think I'm an A-class bitch or something.

"You won't be rude to her," Lisa says. "You'll just explain that she's not exactly what you were looking for."

I scoff. "Apparently, she was what I was looking for this afternoon."

"A quickie." Lisa laughs and adds. "Okay, just send her a message telling her that you thought it over and you're not ready to commit to anyone right now. I mean, unless you *want* to see her again."

"Not really," I say. "Now that I think about it, I don't see her as a long-term Domme for me. I want the real deal." I pause for a moment and add, "Like you have."

"I got lucky," Lisa says, her voice soft. "What do you want in a Domme?"

"The million-dollar question. I want sex, of course."

Lisa laughs. "We all do, darlin'."

"Umm, well, maybe someone to guide me, nurture me, tell me what to do?"

"Yeah, and all of that is not Goddess Fuktard."

"I know. Mommy Tatiana thought I was a *little* and that I needed a Mommy caregiver."

"A *little*? You? I don't get *little* tendencies from you, but you're exploring, so explore away. Just don't commit before running it by me first."

"I won't," I tell her, and mean it.

"You know that you don't have to justify what you think you want to me, B. I don't kink shame. And you know what else?"

"What?"

"I don't know if you watch porn, but that's an interesting place to find out what you like. Find out what turns you on."

"Your stories turn me on. The Domme doles out punishment to a sub, but the sub trusts her so much that it's really not a punishment at all."

"Right, it's a *fun*-ishment. And thanks for the compliment on my stories."

"You know what, Lisa? I want a long-term monogamous relationship with someone who helps me explore my kinks while I help her explore hers. She bolsters me when I need it, and I bolster her."

"I get that. I do," Lisa says. "Hey, I have an idea. Why don't you journal? You've seen the stuff people post on *Kinks*. Maybe you could write out your experiences or write about how you feel at the end of the weekend. Or, or, or," she says as if she's just come up with the most fabulous idea in the world, "why don't you write about the kinks you want to explore. That might attract someone who can help you with that."

"Maybe," I say, knowing she can hear the skepticism in my voice. "I don't know."

"That's okay, B. Just think about it. Sleep on it." She laughs and says, "If I were your Mommy Domme, I would make it your assignment to journal about what you think you want."

"Well, I'm glad you're not my Mommy then. But, Lisa?"

"Yeah?"

"Thanks for the advice. I almost got myself in serious trouble."

"Yeah, you almost did. Glad I was here for you."

"All right, I should let you go," I say, suddenly exhausted.

"You got it, friend," she says. "And think about journaling."

"I will."

We say our goodbyes, and then I decide that I will message Goddess Julie tomorrow, even though her deadline is going to come and go. Lisa's idea of sleeping on big things is good advice. I will take it.

But before I head to bed, I decide to click on the *Journals* icon and search for Mommy Dommes. Just for research, I tell myself. As I peruse the journal posts and stories, most of them are about boy *littles* with Mommy caregivers. And a lot of it is sexual. Not a single one of the things I read is about pedophilia, thank God. I would not be able to handle that. A Big/*little* relationship seems to be along the same lines as a Dominant/submissive relationship, but the Dominant is primarily a caregiver as opposed to a Master or Mistress.

"Or a Goddess," I say and laugh out loud. "A Mommy, Goddess Julia is not."

I read a dozen or more writings to see if I find aspects of myself in these strangers' words. And I do.

One journal post says that Mommies are in charge like a boss and a disciplinarian. She sets up rules and protocols and doles out punishments and reprimands. But what makes them different than a general dominant is that she is the only grown-up in the relationship. She is a caregiver with a soft, nurturing, caring side who uses rules to guide her *little*. She is not a sadistic ruler of the relationship. I would like that. Someone who is not selfish like Goddess Julie seems to be.

I read a few posts that talk about Mommy/*littles* in which there is no sexual play at all. I can't wrap my brain around that concept. One *little* describes her relationship with her Mommy as a person she goes to for comfort when she's anxious and for advice when she's confused. She says that her Mommy has wisdom and experience that she doesn't yet have and doesn't know if she'll ever have.

That's exactly how I feel. Like there are big blank spots of life that I'm missing or can't figure out how to handle. Jen, for instance. We broke up, and yet she's living in my house, and I'm living in this crappy three-story walkup with laundry in the basement. How did that happen? If I'd had a Mommy, it wouldn't have happened. And then there's my teaching position at the college. Somehow, I have yet to convince Dr. Wainwright that I am a serious mathematician who is being wasted teaching first-year courses. I want to delve into theory with serious students who genuinely want to study mathematics. A Mommy might help me figure out how to do that.

I read a few shorter posts by *littles* who want to be dressed up by their Mommies and shown off as cute. Pacifiers, glitter, and coloring pervade these posts, but that's not my gig. I prefer sudoku anyway. I want a strong authoritarian, and I want a relationship where it's not all about me but is sometimes about me. I also want to help my Domme make her life better somehow.

I yawn because it's getting late. I've been at this for a few hours already. I am about to power down *Kinks* and the laptop when a journal title catches my eye. I smile because the writer is a tomboy, just like me.

10 Things Mama Does for her Tomboy
1. Calls me sweetie and tells me I'm a good girl
2. Leaves wake-up texts when she's away on business
3. Lets me rest my head in her lap while we watch *Supergirl*
4. Tucks me in with Mr. McCuddles
5. Tells me she's proud of me
6. Knows when I'm upset and knows when I need to talk something out
7. Listens to my secrets

8. Offers guidance and teaches life lessons
9. Enforces rules with discipline when I need it
10. Loves me

"Loves me," I quote. "Tells me I'm a good girl." Yes, I do want those things, but does that make me a *little*? Do I want a Mommy? A caregiver?

The questions take over my brain as I power down the laptop and get ready for bed. Earlier, Lisa asked me to figure out what I wanted, and some things have become uber-clear. I want to be noticed, needed, and nurtured. And appreciated, too. Wait. What about love? Yes, yes, yes. I want that, too, and maybe I've just given myself permission to seek out and find all of those things.

Thoughts of Goddess Julie are far away as I fall asleep, imagining that someone called Mommy is tucking me in, kissing my forehead, and telling me she's proud of me and that I'm a good girl.

Chapter 5

Never Say Never

Goddess Julie's message is one word. It says, "Hmm." That's it. I've barely got one eye open and take another sip of coffee to steel my nerves before I write my return message.

As calmly as I can, I type, "I have decided that I am not looking for the kind of relationship that you are offering." My fingers hover over the keyboard. What else? What else? Should I thank her for the sex yesterday? I have no idea how to do that without sounding like an idiot. Should I wish her luck?

"C'mon, Bernadette," I say out loud, "finish it." Fine, fine. I hit send. That's it. Short and sweet. Lisa would be proud.

I tap the lid to my laptop closed and get up. I'm taking myself out for breakfast and Christmas shopping, even though I don't have anyone here in Cincinnati to buy for anymore. Not since I broke up with Jen, and my supposed friends abandoned me. And this year, I want to do more than exchange gift cards with my brother, his wife, and Dad. I want to find meaningful gifts to show them I've thought about them.

I'm dressed and out the door in minutes. Rocco's, my favorite truck stop dive near the Interstate, isn't too busy, thank goodness. I am not up for a crowd this morning. I settle in and perk up when I see Marlene, my favorite waitress, coming over. Her face lights up when she sees me. She's middle aged and one of those people who make you feel seen.

"Haven't seen you here in a while, Professor." She pours coffee into my cup without asking and dumps a mountain of creamers on the table in front of me. "Staying out of trouble?" She winks to tell me she's teasing.

"Never." And this time, it's the truth.

"Good for you. What'll you have, hun?"

35

I order my usual – cheese omelet, home fries, white bread toast, and a chocolate shake. I tell her the shake is to go. When she leaves the table, I resist the urge to get out my phone and see if Goddess Julie has replied or flamed my inbox or something. Instead, I breathe deep and wonder what it would be like to have a Mommy Domme.

How would you have sex? It would be weird, wouldn't it? But wait, wait, wait. This isn't age play. This isn't me thinking I'm a child or pretending to be a child. No, this is me at age thirty-two, wanting a strong woman who's authoritarian and strict but who is also nurturing and kind and has my best interests at heart. A woman who is no-nonsense and mothering and helps me navigate troubling spots in my grown-up life. And I can also help and support and give her whatever she needs because it's about that, too.

Not that I'm attracted to Marlene, because I'm not, but she's a caregiving mothering type. She brings me comfort. There's a reason she has a lot of regular customers. There are a lot of lonely people out there, and you can tell just by looking at the number of tables in this truck stop with just one person, including mine. Like me, I imagine they're grateful to a person like Marlene who dotes on them, if only for a little while.

I always give Marlene a big tip, and today is no exception. As I'm leaving, she says, "Take care of yourself, hun."

"I will," I answer back. And then I chuckle because I'm trying to find someone who will help me do just that.

I head to a big box department store and find a few things for my family for Christmas. I get a sweater for Dad, along with a pair of minion glasses that'll make him look goofy. He'll appreciate the silliness. And then, for Jordan and Cathy, I get a Keurig coffee pot with a carafe that they'd been hinting for. When I get home, I'll order them a subscription to one of those once-a-month specialty coffee deliveries. I also pick up a few Christmas decorations for my measly apartment. The rest of my decorations are still in the attic at my house. I find a whopping one-foot-tall fake Christmas tree with tiny lights already on it, a wreath for my apartment door, and a snowperson with a cute expression, mainly because it reminds me of Mom. Since I can't afford to fly home this year, I also buy a box for mailing the gifts.

As I drive home with my purchases, my heart squeezes at the changes my life has taken over recent years. Mom's cancer and her passing. Dad moving in with Jordan and Cathy. Me moving to Cincinnati, far away from family and friends. Maybe Dr. Wainwright's inability to see my worth is the wake-up call I need to move back to California. I make a mental note to research associate professorship positions back home. Yes, maybe that's what this girl needs. A change in environment. But it was that longing for a change in environment that made me move away in the first place. I'm as confused as ever as I drive home.

I take one trip up the three flights with all my bags, and I'm a bit winded when I finally get inside my apartment. "Phew, you've gotta get in shape, girl," I say to myself. Would a Mommy help me with that? I groan. I really do have a one-track mind. I need to chill out and put up my decorations, wrap the presents, and then box them up to mail tomorrow between classes.

I pour some wine, and I throw on some Christmas music using my Pandora app. I sing along while I decorate and wrap. Throughout it all, the ache in my chest is still there. I wish I had someone to decorate with me. Someone to hold the ladder while I string my old-school C9 Christmas lights on the house gutters. But then again, I don't live there anymore.

Deflated, I collapse in the chair at my desk and turn off the music. I absolutely know the best way to relax and fire up my laptop. Where is it? Where is it? Ahh, here we go. Here's how to get real life off my mind. Lisa wanted me to watch porn, so watch porn, I will. I click on the saved title, *Domme Plays with Her submissive.*

The scene takes a few minutes to get going, so that gives me time to check the locks and the curtains before disrobing in the living room. I give the thermostat a quick tweak up so that I won't freeze, and I'm back at my desk pulling out supplies.

The dark-haired Domme on the screen is a little older than her blonde submissive. She has a crop in her hand. Yeesh, why is a crop so sexy? Is it the power it yields? Or how it emphasizes the power difference between the two women? The Domme is wearing a low-back strapless bustier. It's black and sexy as hell when her long, dark hair falls over her shoulders. I lean back and watch as the Domme lifts the sub's loose t-shirt to reveal her breasts underneath.

"You're not wearing a bra, Antonia," the Domme

37

admonishes.

"No, Ma'am." She looks away, embarrassed.

"And look at those nipples. So hard." The Domme taps each nipple in turn with the crop. The sub gasps both times. "Such a naughty girl."

"Yes, Ma'am," the sub says, but this time her expression is coquettish.

The Domme pulls down the cups of her bustier while her sub watches, revealing beautifully rounded breasts ripe for the picking. With the crop still in her hand, she rubs her fingers over her own nipples, hardening them.

The sub's expression is priceless. It looks like she cannot wait to get those perfect nipples in her mouth.

Using both hands, the Domme lifts and squeezes her right breast, offering it to her sub. The sub leans forward, revealing her hands cuffed together behind her back.

A shot of lust runs through me. I absolutely want to be the blonde sub in the video. Take away my decisions and tell me what to do. Use me how you want to.

As if starved, the sub hungrily sucks and licks her Domme's nipples alternating from right to left as they are offered. She occasionally glances up at her Domme as if looking for approval or maybe praise for a job well done.

"I would do the same, honey," I say to the sub. I rub my own nipples and squirm at the delightful connection between them and my southland. I reach into the bag on my desk and take out six clothespins. One for each nipple and four more for other places that I'll figure out later.

The first pin goes on my first nipple gloriously. I bask in the pulsing pain as I watch the drama unfolding on my laptop.

> The Domme leans back on the couch. She makes a slow and sexy show of pulling off her black lace panties and then twirls them around her finger before letting them fly off camera. She definitely has her sub's attention. She helps the sub, whose hands are still cuffed behind her, lean forward until the sub's face is inches from the Domme's pussy. The Domme uses her fingers to part her perfectly pink lips in invitation.

> The sub wastes no time, leans forward, and starts licking.

> Using the hand still holding the crop, the Domme grabs the sub's head and holds her tight.

Oh, God. I want to run my hands down my body and touch myself, but I hold off. I have more clips to attach. My second nipple is just as sensitive as the first, and I moan at the combination of pain and pleasure. My hand has a mind of its own and leaves a sexy trail down my body. I imagine it is a Domme trailing her fingers across my skin. No, it's her crop.

I grab two more clothespins. There is a closeup of the sub slowly and artfully licking her Domme's pussy on the screen. The zoomed-in shot of the Domme's erect clit is nothing short of artful. It's so big. I imagine pulling it into my mouth and sucking on it like a straw, running my hardened tongue across the tip and then up and down the sides. I run imaginary circles around the base and then pull it into my mouth again. Another shot of lust hits me, and I attach two clothespins to my fleshy outer lips. Two more join the others. I flick the pins on my breasts, causing a delightful highway of sensation down below. I flick the lower pins, enjoying the naughtiness of my actions.

"Are you trying to make me cum, Antonia?" the Domme

on the screen asks.

"Yes, Ma'am," Antonia says, barely taking a break from her task.

"I didn't tell you to make me cum. I just wanted you to bathe my pussy."

Despite the Domme's words, the sub continues licking. Her head bobs back and forth as she works.

"You must be punished for acting without permission, Antonia."

Antonia sits up and frowns. She's obviously upset because her Domme is disappointed in her.

"Assume the position."

Antonia, her hands still cuffed behind her, shimmies off the couch and leans over the armrest. Her ass sticks up in the air.

The Domme sucks air in between her clenched teeth. "Ah, such a beautiful canvas on which to paint." She rubs a hand over one ass cheek and then the other. The first few blows from the crop are almost tender, just a warm-up. This Domme knows how to wield the crop because her technique is smooth and fluid. The sub groans as the strikes get harder.

"Let's get into a rhythm now," the Domme says. She thwacks her sub with three medium strikes, counting, "One, two, three." And then three harder, more intense strikes, "Four, five, six." She repeats the cadence several more times and then says, "One more time, Antonia. Four, five, and six will be the hardest yet." Four, five, and six sound and look like they really hurt.

"Thank you, Ma'am," Antonia says breathlessly. Her previously white ass is pulsing red and hot. It is a beautiful sight and truly does represent an artist's canvas.

"And *now* you have permission to make me cum, Antonia." The Domme moves around and puts one knee on the couch in front of her sub's face. She arches her pelvis. The close-up shot shows how sloppy wet the Domme is.

The sub pushes her tongue out and eagerly licks the woman who just whacked her repeatedly with a crop.

I can't hold back any longer and plunge two fingers into my pussy. I thrust in and out, delighting at the pain from the clothespins as my wrist pushes past them. With my other hand, I rake some of the wetness onto my clit to lubricate it. It doesn't take long before the spark of a building orgasm hits me. I plunge my fingers back in but stop for a moment. I love this heightened feeling and don't want it to end too soon. I also want to cum when the Domme cums. I push down on the pins clamping my nipples, and moan. Pain is so fucking good. Oh, my God.

I pull my fingers out of my pussy slowly and ram them back in. Slow ascent, ramming descent. I pick up the pace as the Domme throws her head back and bucks her hips against her sub's face.

"Yes, Antonia. Yes. Good fucking pussy sucker."

I imagine she's talking to me and that I'm the one sucking on her pussy. I rub my clit with lighting speed, and my distant orgasm takes the bullet train and explodes. My pussy clamps down around my fingers as I moan my release. I continue to thrust, remembering how Mistress Ciara and her BBC kept up the motion after I came the first time. I purposely thwack into the four clothespins down below. Oh, God, I feel it. Holy shit. Another one is forming. The second train is in the tunnel, its white light speeding toward me. The bright light hits my soul, and I cum again. My heart pounds, my pussy pulses, and the pain points throb. I pull my fingers out and wipe the wetness on my stomach. On the screen, the Domme cums and gasps praise-filled words to her sub. I want a Domme like that. Yes, yes, yes.

I'm about to reach down and undo the clothespins when I realize I wiped my cum-soaked fingers over the words *Goddess Julie's* written on my stomach. The words are smeared. Good. I dip my fingers back in for more of the viscous wetness and wipe more of her name off my body. It's fitting, I think. My cum erasing her out of my life.

My breathing slows down, and it's time to take the pins off. Slowly, one by one, I unclip them. A jolt of pain accompanies each one. But it's a delicious pain. I still don't understand the pain-to-pleasure connection, but I know that it's real.

I get up and wash my hands and then clean the six clothespins in hot hot water in the kitchen sink before putting them on a dry towel on the counter. I need a new towel on my desk chair, too. That one is soaked through. I'll bring one back after I shower. Aah, yes, a shower to scrub the rest of Goddess Julie's name off my body and out of my life. But curiosity gets me, and I have to check if she's responded to my break-up message. I really don't want to seem rude or have her be mad at me.

I click open the mail icon but don't see our message folder. Lisa's message folder is there, and I'm confused. Where the heck are the messages to and from Goddess Julie?

I figuratively scratch my head and type in *Goddess Julie* in the *Kinks* search engine. Nothing comes up. I type in *Goddess,* and a ton of profile names come up, but not hers. What is going on?

I blow out a confused sigh and shrug. Oh, well. At least she's gone. I message Lisa and tell her how I answered Goddess Julie and how I can't find my message folder from her anymore.

Lisa gets back to me right away and says matter-of-factly, "She blocked your ass, Bernadette."

I'm shocked. Blocked? Me? I wasn't rude or mean to her. Why would she do that to me? I'm so nice.

Lisa says, "Welcome to the world of *Kinks.com*, B. It comes with the territory. Get used to it. One day it'll be you blocking some asshat."

I hate to think that I would ever do that to someone, but I've learned never to say never.

Chapter 6
Stimulus-response

The rest of Sunday afternoon flies by with satisfying tasks like thoroughly scrubbing off Goddess Julie's name in the shower, dressing in loose sweats, and putting the last touches on the final exams I'll be giving this week. Printable copies are due to Miss Olga tomorrow at eight a.m., but I know she will appreciate mine sitting in her email in-box when she arrives. She has to have time to make enough copies. She always complains about how my colleagues submit their exams late or not at all, and she has to go running around doing their jobs for them.

As I microwave my Hungry Hamlet meal, I muse on Miss Olga. She's such a Mommy type caregiver. That's why I gravitated toward her, isn't it? She takes care of the other administrative assistants, and she takes care of me. I wonder if anyone thinks it's weird that I regularly have lunch with the administrative assistants. If so, too bad. I like the comfort they give me. And knowing that Miss Olga has my back in all things, I decide to push for an appointment with Dr. Wainwright. A week ago, I called and left a message on his voicemail telling him I wanted a meeting to discuss courses, but he never got back to me. This time I send an email directly to Miss Olga. She will make darn sure I get on his schedule.

I mean, I know I'm the youngest and the newest member of the department, but I've been here for five years already. Haven't I put in my time at the bottom yet? I have the two courses with the largest enrollments. In the least, I deserve recognition for handling those, but what I really want is to move up. I want to teach higher courses. I want to teach post-grad students. I haven't done much research concerning group theory beyond my dissertation, which aggravates me to no end. It's time I got out of the freshman business and moved onto some serious mathematics where I can have breathing room, graduate student assistants, and research time.

I bring my meal to my desk and laugh because I live at this desk. All kinds of things happen here. I grade papers, eat meals, drink wine, and play with myself. I feel a twinge of embarrassment at the last one, which is odd because I've had sex with strangers on the internet and even drove to another city to have an orgy with several strangers. I try not to think of the million things that could have gone horribly wrong about that trip to Columbus because I would be appalled at myself for being so slutty and careless. Perhaps my newfound love of lust should stay hidden beneath the surface. Perhaps I should keep these desires and yearnings of mine to myself and never let them out again. The problem is that so many other people have similar desires, which tells me that mine aren't out of the ordinary. My fantasies and cravings aren't wrong. Oh, sure, there are tons of things on *Kinks* that I wouldn't do, but who am I to say that others shouldn't explore those things? Ah, the yin-yang of it all.

I finish my microwaved fast food and firmly decide that microwaved French fries suck. I will try reheating them in the oven next time. Oh, but how am I going to wait those extra ten minutes?

I laugh out loud and decide that's what I need more in my life. No, not French fries. Patience. I click open *Kinks,* hit up the journal writing portion of the website, and write up some thoughts about the yin-yang of BDSM.

> Yin-Yang: Two complementary forces. The yang starts an action, the yin reacts to it. This creates balance. But the act of finishing is also an action, and this action then requires a re-action. And the cycle continues.

> The yang of day starts the cycle, the yin of night finishes it. The pitcher's yang starts, the catcher's yin finishes. The yang of a Dominant's actions starts, the submissive's yin finishes it, completing one cycle for both.

> Without the yang of Dominance, there is no yin of submission. Without the yin of submission, there is no yang of Dominance.

I post my journal for all on *Kinks* to see, but I don't expect anyone to find it or comment. Crafting the post has calmed me somewhat. Focusing on a concept and putting my thoughts together helps me feel grounded. And feeling grounded helps me decide that it's okay to explore some Mommy/*little-girl* groups. I had to do a bit of internet definition searching for the group called "MD/lg" and find out that it stands for Mommy Domme/*little-girl*. Great, this one is specifically for women. I can't say for sure that it's a group of lesbians because all kinds of things go on in the *Kinks* world. And sure enough, when I explore the visitors' section of the group, I see that many of the pairings are heterosexual women who are not sexual with each other, just nurturing. Some pairings have other partners, too. I don't want those kinds of relationships. I want a lesbian partner. Or she can be bisexual, of course, but I want a monogamous partner who wants to not only love and nurture me but who also wants to drape me over her lovely couch and have her way with me.

I fondly remember being draped over Mistress Ciara's kitchen table. The bruises have finally faded, but the memories have not. Mistress Ciara never offered me love or nurturing. I have to have all three – loving, nurturing, *and* draping.

I click on the join button and answer their screening question. I tell them about my newly-discovered/newly-admitted submissive side and my desire to explore MD/lg relationships. I also say that I think I am more of a *middle* than a *little*. *Middles*, I've come to discover, are older and not inclined to want pacifiers or blankies or glitter or crayons. That's not me. But the need to hide in a caregiver's shoulder when something is scary? Absolutely.

I don't hear back from the group right away, so I decide to channel some ideas into another journal post. The words flow freely and quickly.

> *Littles* and *Middles*: When I first learned about *littles*, I didn't understand the concept. I didn't realize it was a real *thing*. Honestly, I thought it was merely role-playing. Coloring books, stuffies, cartoons. Seemed silly to me. It seemed like play-acting to get attention. Until I realized that it *was* real and that it might be what I am. It

was like finally putting a name to how I had been feeling for a long, long time.

The label *little* doesn't quite fit me, though. But perhaps *middle* does. I sleep with a Pooh bear, always have. I like the DC Comics shows. I'd much rather play in the yard, run around, throw my line in the water, and climb a tree. I guess we all long for those carefree days of youth, and that's all I thought it was.

The more I meditate about it, the more I realize that I am still there at that time of my life. In my mind, anyway. I am "stuck" emotionally at around the time my life got scary. And that was right around puberty and discovering that I liked girls, even though I was supposed to like icky boys. And, actually, boys weren't icky; they were teammates and sports partners. But the boys didn't really accept me as one of their own. And neither did the girls. My parents called me a tomboy. Still am. I guess nowadays, I would label myself a boi or maybe even non-binary.

I'm not sure about those labels, and they may fit, but all I know is that I think I need a caregiver, an understanding one. Someone who will listen as I try to make sense of the world around me. Someone who will tell me that I don't have to be *big* "if I'm not ready." Someone who will help me see things that I, for whatever reason, cannot see or don't understand.

Please don't get me wrong and think that I am a mindless child. I can fake being *Big*. I've done it my whole life. I have a Ph.D. in an academic field, and I do many *Big* things, but inside? Inside, I think I am still that 11-year-old tomboy trying to figure out where I fit into this world.

So, for me, being a *middle* might be a real thing. And now I have to figure out what that means.

I post this second journal piece and wait. I'm not exactly sure what I'm waiting for, but I realized that I have gobs of patience for certain things in my life, like the patience to teach the lower-level courses I am coming to resent. But tonight, I have absolutely no patience as I wait to be accepted into the MD/lg group and no patience waiting for people to comment on or like my posted journals.

Fine. I'll do something else. I grab my phone and power up my e-reader app. There is a certain slave girl named Five I left exposing herself to a couple of randy lesbians on a couch. Now, what in the world are they up to? Ah, speaking of couches, I need a change of scenery. I plop myself on my own lovely secondhand couch with a pillow under my head and several towels under my body and settle in.

> The two women on the couch continued their banter, but a silent signal from Ma'am told me to circulate around the large open-concept living room. A strikingly attractive dark-skinned woman about Ma'am's age sat by herself in one of Ma'am's wingback chairs. She wore the shortest skirt I'd ever seen and thigh-high stockings with garter belts disappearing under the skirt. Her tight blouse accentuated her cleavage, and I found myself salivating. Ma'am has conditioned us to become highly aroused at sights like this, and I felt my breathing become labored. Oh, how I wish I could speak. I would tell this woman how attractive and sexy she was. And if that wasn't enough, she reached down and smiled at me before brushing a stray lock of hair out of my eyes.

> "You are a lovely drink cart, little one. Perhaps after the couch twins have their way with you, I'll use your tongue

to please me. Would you like that?"

I nodded once but couldn't help the small smile that crept onto my face. I looked down immediately, feeling my cheeks get overly warm.

"That's a good girl," she said and then took a drink from the cooler on my back. After opening it, she patted my butt and said, "Off you go, little girl." And I did.

The next two women I approached paid absolutely no attention to me, so I moved on to another group who took a couple of drinks from my cooler but also pretty much ignored me. Soon enough, my route took me back to the couch twins, Bobbie and the Dame.

Before they could touch me again, Ma'am stood in front of me. If I didn't have this blasted cooler strapped to my back, I would have leaned down to kiss her feet. She must have understood that and offered me her hand instead. I kissed and kissed and kissed her hand, tearing up as I did so. Oh, how much I loved her. She was so good to me and the other girls. She understood the love and affection we craved, but she also understood the firm discipline we needed. She was perfect.

"Open," she said.

I stopped kissing her hand, opened my mouth, and lifted my chin to allow her access. She placed a drinking straw between my lips and said, "Drink. You'll need to stay hydrated while you service my guests. Do you understand?"

I nodded once and kept drinking as long as the straw was

there. She pulled the straw away, and I dropped my gaze.

"Open," she said, "and stay open." This time, instead of a straw, she placed two fingers in my mouth. She rested them on my tongue, not quite far enough to cause my gag reflex. "Relax, Five." I hadn't realized that I'd tensed up. I guess I still need training. Her fingers remained in my mouth, and I used the technique she'd taught me to relax. I visibly pictured my muscles relaxing one by one, and in no time at all, her fingers on my tongue seemed like the most natural thing in the world to me.

"Pull my fingers in." We'd done this exercise a few times before, but never in front of guests. I pulled my tongue back, and her fingers rode along. She liked me to hold them back there for a moment while she twirled her fingers around the boundaries of the far reaches of my mouth. "Continue to relax, please."
I did so, relishing her touch in such an intimate part of my body, relishing this quiet demonstration of her power and possessiveness over me. I couldn't help but notice that the couch twins were still and quiet as they watched my Ma'am work me. I felt immense pride and tried not to get emotional. Ma'am moved her fingers then. She rubbed my tongue from back to front and then side to side as if petting me. Her fingers tasted wonderful; they tasted like her. Too soon, she pulled them out. "Close," she said. Disappointed, I closed my mouth and then looked down. Ma'am wiped her hands on a wet rag offered to her by Two and then took the tray provided by One.

"Now, Five," she said, "these are the toys that my guests might use on and in your body. You're here for their pleasure."

I nodded once to let her know that I had seen the toys and that I understood. I felt arousal weep from my pussy, and I wondered if anyone else saw it, too. Probably not. They're drooling over the assortment of toys on the tray. These are exclusively *my* toys. You can tell by the number 5 stamped or carved on each one. Even the metal Ben Wa balls have been laser etched with 5s. None of the other girls have ever had my toys in their bodies. Ma'am tries her best to keep us healthy, even requiring her guests to show proof of testing before coming to one of her parties.

Ma'am sets the tray down on a side table and then stands up tall. She takes the bell offered to her by One and rings it like she's ringing school into session. A cheer goes up in the space, and Ma'am says, "Let the fun begin."

The Dame was up instantly. "Nipple clips, for sure."

"Abso-fuckin-lutely," Bobbie said in her rough and tumble voice. "I'll let you do the honors."

Thank you," the Dame said. "Ahh, look here, Bobbie. Ben Wa balls." She lifted one off the tray and shook it. Sarah loved to hear the chimes ring, especially when Ma'am put them inside her and then used her strap-on to push it in further. They would ring out from deep inside Sarah's womb. "One or two?"

"Let's go with one," Bobbie said. "I can make it ring. I'm going deep tonight."

Strong fingers pinched first one nipple and then the other. The Dame pulled Sarah's nipples down one after

51

the other as if she were milking a cow. While the Dame was doing that, Bobbie's fingers pulled Sarah's inner pussy lips wide apart. The cold Ben Wa ball touched Sarah's skin, and then Bobbie pushed it inside as far as her fingers could reach. "Keep that in there, slave," she said to Sarah from behind. Sarah nodded once and used her pelvic muscles to suck the ball in even further. Her internal muscles were powerful because Ma'am had them exercise those particular muscles practically every day.

Without warning, the Dame clamped one of Sarah's nipples with a clip. Sarah inhaled sharply but made no other sound. She was a bit more ready for the second clip and didn't inhale as violently. The Dame let the chain between the two clips dangle freely.

Sarah enjoyed the pulsing pain of her now-throbbing nipples as the two women picked over the toy tray, discussing strap-on lengths and girths. The Dame preferred a "pretty pink one," while Bobbie seemed to go for the largest one there. It wasn't long before the Dame told Sarah to open up and presented the pretty pink dildo to her mouth. "Just a warmup, little fuck cart, isn't it? Soon you'll be sucking my clit, won't you?" The words sounded so inviting, especially delivered with her English accent.

Sarah couldn't nod her head this time because the Dame had started a nice rhythm in her mouth. Sarah tried to provide just the right amount of suction as the Dame fucked her mouth. Pleasing Ma'am's guests was the goal of the evening – so Sarah tried to do just that. Out of the corner of her eye, Sarah saw One draped over an older woman's lap and spanked. Her ass cheeks were already bright red. Sarah was happy because One craved a heavy hand.

It wasn't long before Bobbie's gargantuan dildo pushed at the entrance to Sarah's pussy. Her hopes for a spanking or a paddling were dashed as Bobbie slowly pushed into her. Bobbie's dildo filled Sarah completely, and the metal Ben Wa ball bumped up against her cervix. Bobbie then grabbed both of Sarah's hips and started a gentle cadence. It was obvious that these two women had double-teamed a slave before because Sarah melted like butter between them.

Sarah felt a stimulus-response building deep in her body. Ma'am called it an *SR*. She taught her slaves that orgasms were what Dominants had, and slaves merely had a response to the Dominant's stimulus. An *SR* was a way for the slave to show appreciation for the Dominant's actions on their bodies. A slave's wet and spasming pussy was the ultimate tribute to the Dominant. Oh, sure, occasionally, she told them to hold back their *SRs*, but that was only to train them in case she or one of her guests required this. Typically, though, she wanted her slaves to have as many *SRs* as they could.

Ma'am's slaves were never ever to play with each other unless Ma'am or a guest asked. And then they were to remember that they were only stimulating each other for the Dominant's enjoyment. If the Dominant wanted them to have an *SR*, then they absolutely could and should.

Laying on my couch, I moan at the story's images flitting through my brain. "Stimulus-response," I say out loud. I slide my fingers through my slit. "Orgasms are for Dommes, not me," I murmur. "I am a slave."

53

I sit up and get on my knees in front of the couch, using a pillow under my knees. My phone with Sarah's story has fallen out of reach on the floor, but it doesn't matter. Imaginary Bobbie's dildo is sliding in and out of me, and my only purpose is to please the couch twins. To let them use my body any way they want to. That is my job as a slave. Ma'am will be pleased with me. If I have an *SR*, it is only to please my superiors. What I want doesn't matter.

The dildo speeds up inside me. I have no chiming Ben Wa balls, but I put them on my mental list of things to buy. I feel an SR building. It is of no consequence; My Dommes' orgasms and their pleasures are all that matter. I press my shoulders into the couch and lay my head on the cushions as she pummels me from behind. "Take it like the slave you are," imaginary Bobbie says to me. Her stimulus makes me respond, and it is snowballing. "I like using your body, slave. I pull you back and forth with my hands, gripping your hips. That cooler is heavy, isn't it, fuck cart? Ice sloshing all over your body." I can almost feel the cold wetness on my skin. "Feel me slide in and out of you, slave."

The words ignite my *SR,* and I fall over the brink. My inner walls grip her dildo, making it hard for her to thrust. "Excellent, slave. Well-trained response," she mutters to me. I keep thrusting the dildo in and out, milking the *SR* for all it's worth. I am proud that I gave such a lovely tribute to the imaginary Dommes. "Oh, but I need one more tribute, slave," Bobbie demands of me. She continues to pound me, and I imagine I hear the chimes from inside my body as she smashes against the Ben Wa ball. "I want to hear you cry out in gratitude that I bothered to notice you, slave, let alone use your body for my enjoyment." My ass rises in the air, and my knees spread wide and fall off the pillow onto the carpeting. The rug burns hurt, but I don't care. My Domme's comfort and enjoyment are the only things that matter.

Another *SR* builds. This one is close.

I love to moan, but Sarah can't, so I won't either. It hits, and I open my mouth wide and exhale all the air out of my body. I gasp air quickly. I ride each spasm without a sound other than my breathing. I am still gasping as the dildo slows and then slides out. I fall onto my back and lay panting on the floor for a few moments, my legs spread wide. I finally catch my breath and feel cool air on the veritable puddle between my legs, but I don't care. My imaginary Domme is so pleased that she tells me I am a good girl. She tells me that my two *SRs* are a beautiful homage to her.

"Thank you for the honor of serving you, Ma'am," I say out loud. My eyes close by themselves. I am asleep within moments.

Chapter 7
Do They?

For some reason, I'm in a good mood as I sit in my office at the university Monday morning. Miss Olga must have gotten here super early because she set up an appointment for me to see Dr. Wainwright first thing Wednesday morning. I knew she'd come through for me.

I have successfully answered the endless emails that managed to pile up over the weekend, the bulk of them from students wanting extra credit opportunities. A good old cut-and-pasted message about our department's policy about no extra credit gets sent to every one of them. Oh, a few braver students will eventually show up at my office door to beg in person, and my answer is always some version of "too little, too late," "where were you during the semester?" or "I can't do the work for you." Too much gets handed to young people these days. But it's not me being a bitch; it really is the department's policy.

I jump when there's a knock on my closed door. Ahh, here we go. Let the begging begin. "Come," I say to the unknown person on the other side of the door and instantly regret my choice of word.

The door opens tentatively, and a student walks in.

"Oh, hey," I say to the young woman I had seen at the DIY store on Saturday. She's a little bit older than my usual 18- or 19-year-old students, maybe somewhere in her mid-twenties, but that doesn't matter. I make a point of never getting into my students' personal lives. I barely know their names anyway. They are faces in a lecture hall and names on a roster. Rarely do I put the two together. Maybe I should start doing that. All of that goes through my head as the young woman sits down on the other side of my desk. "What can I do for you?"

"I'm nervous for Wednesday," she says and grimaces.

"The exam?"

"Mm hmm."

"Have you kept up with the work?" I ask because I have no idea what kind of student she is.

"I've tried to. It's just, you know, a lot of stuff. I've been doing a ton of practice problems, though." She pulls a spiral notebook out of her backpack. "I've had trouble trying to figure out where to start on a few of these. Do you mind helping me?"

"Let's do it. I love math." This makes her laugh, and I make room for her to place her chair next to mine at my desk. There is no room in my closet of an office to work with students any other way.

"I feel dumb asking for help. I mean, I'm Asian." She gestures to her obvious Asian ethnicity. "And supposedly, I have a math gene." She laughs and adds, "But it sure doesn't feel like it."

I chuckle, not quite knowing what to say. "Okay, hit me."

We spend the next fifteen minutes or so clearing up her confusion about the average value of a function versus the average rate of change of a function. I make sure that she does most of the work as we do the problems so I can verify that she does, indeed, understand.

"Your algebra is quite good," I tell her. "And these notes are impeccable." She's copied my lecture notes down to a T, even the joke I made about Calculus students being teetotalers because they shouldn't drink and derive. I feel awkward that I still don't know her name. "Looks like you write down practically everything I said. That's great."

She laughs. "I review the notes when I get home." She covers her eyes with her hand, obviously embarrassed, and her sleeve pulls up.

"Oh, I love your bracelet." I can't believe those words have just come out of my mouth. If that wasn't bad enough, the next few are worse. "Is that a triskelion?" Oh, my God. Why, oh why, can't I keep my mouth shut? I know damn well what that symbol is and what it means.

She quickly pushes it up underneath her sleeve. "Oh, it was a gift from my mistress –" She stops mid-sentence and then says, "a gift from my girlfriend when we made it official."

"That's nice." I leave it at that because to say anything more would get me in trouble. Not meaning to, I clear my throat, giving away my uneasiness.

"Well, it sounds like you have a good grasp on the material now. You should be fine on Wednesday."

"Thank you, Professor Garneau." She stands up and moves the chair back to the far side of my desk. "I appreciate everything you've done for me this semester."

"You're welcome."

"Are you sure you can't teach Calculus Two?"

I chuckle. "We haven't gotten our course load for next semester, but I doubt it." Curiosity gets the better of me, and I say, "What's your major?"

"Oh, uh, I am an Animal Sciences major. I plan to go to veterinary school. Mistress is encouraging me to pursue my dreams, so I…" She trails off as if she realizes the mistake she just made.

I keep a straight face and say, "I think it's great. With your work ethic, you should go as far as you want to go."

"Thank you, Ma'am," she says, her face tinging red to the roots of her dark hair.

"You're welcome," I say. "See you on Wednesday."

When the door closes behind her, I sit at my desk, paralyzed. She called me "Ma'am." Does she think I'm a Domme? I'm an authority figure for her, being a professor and all, but that doesn't make me have a dominant personality. Does she know that I'm exploring? How could she?

I'm grateful that her class is ending and that I will no longer have to interact with her. Oh, she was a nice enough young woman, but it's too dangerous. I'm trying to work my way up to better and more lucrative courses here, not get fired for being a pervert.

I laugh. People take great pride in calling themselves perverts on *Kinks*. I'm not sure I'm there with them yet. However, some ideas have been marinating in my brain since I fell asleep on the living room floor last night. I woke up about an hour later, cold as hell. A quick shower, warm jammies, and a snuggly bed put me in just the right frame of mind to dream about having a Mommy. Ideas for another journal post have been swirling in my mind all morning. Since I can't use my laptop at the university, I go old school and take out a perforated writing pad to write down ideas. I write a tentative title, "Mommy Needed for a *Middle* Tomboy," and then scribble down my thoughts that come faster than I can get them down. I write in the margins and the headers and footers, and eventually, I have something I feel proud of. I'll type it up as soon as I get home.

Time flies by with a pleasant and cheerful lunch with Miss Olga and the other administrative assistants and then office hours for my Elementary Functions classes after that. There are only two grade beggars that I think I handle adeptly. Once home, I shed my clothes, go to the restroom, and then make myself a cup of hot tea. No wine right now. I have to focus coherently on my latest journal posting. After I post it, I will look to see if the MD/lg group accepted me. But for now, I re-read what I've typed.

> WANTED AD: Mommy Needed for a *Middle* Tomboy. This is how the ad's headline reads in my head, but I haven't the nerve to post it. Is that who I am? Seriously? Am I really a *middle*? The ad's body that rambles through my head always contains something like this: *Middle tomboy needs a Mommy for nurturing and guidance and love and discipline.*

> This *middle* likes sports but also likes school. I do my chores without being told. Okay, that was a big fat lie. I *try* to remember to do my chores, but I will absolutely do them if a Mommy reminds me. And I don't mind taking the garbage and recycling cans to the street. Tomboys don't mind that kind of stuff.

> A Mommy will tuck me in at night, but not every night because I am *not* a *little*, after all. And, of course, as soon as Mommy leaves the room, I'll get out my flashlight and read lesbian fiction under the covers even though Mommy says I shouldn't (but I think she knows. Mommies know everything, don't they?)

> I know that Mommies sometimes need to instill discipline with punishments. It's what Mommies do.

Sex sounds one-part scary and one-part fun. Maybe a Mommy can teach me? I want a Mommy who will pull me into a hug and rock me and say, "It's okay, Crystal. You'll be okay. I won't let anything happen to you. I'll take care of everything."

But this ad running through my head will probably never go up because no Mommies want a pathetic, lonely tomboy who is good at math and likes sports.

Do they?

I read it over, satisfied that it conveys what I want. One time, I typed the name Bernadette but caught it quickly because, on *Kinks*, I am Crystal, not Bernadette. And it's not really an ad, per se, but it kind of is. Maybe someone will notice it. Probably not. A strange sense of calm hits me, so I post it though. With a satisfied nod, I move on and click on my two other journal posts. Ahh, Lisa left nice messages on both. She's so encouraging. A few other people left messages as well. The calm I felt moments ago dissipates into thin air. I can't stop the tightness growing in my shoulders as I wonder if one of these people who responded could be a Mommy figure for me.

Someone named Peace_Y'all said she thought my "Yin-Yang" post was "groovy." Dicks_for_Chicks offered to "yin my yang" anytime. I seriously doubt the erect dick he uses as an avatar is his. I'm sure his is much closer to the size of my pinky. A third comment thanks me for such a thoughtful post. Her name is Strict_Mommy.

Strict_Mommy also left a comment on my second journal post. She says, "It's wonderful to explore. If I can be of any help, please let me know." Oh, I'm sure you can help, I think cynically, just like Goddess Julie helped me.

I cluck my tongue against my teeth in chastisement. "You have no idea who this is, Bernadette. Give her a chance." I roll my eyes but agree with my statement. No judgments. Not yet. But before I jump into scouring Strict_Mommy's page and pictures and profile and kinks, I hit up the MD/lg group. Eureka! I've been accepted. Now it's time to explore this world of Bigs and *littles*.

I find the discussion boards quickly and find a topic titled "Soft Limits – A Contradiction?"

> PAINBECOMESYOU: Soft limits are not contradictions at all. A limit is a boundary. A soft limit is like a rubber fence. It means you're willing to bump up against it to see how it feels.

> MAMA_DECIDES: A hard limit means that limit is pretty much set in stone, and to bump up against it is not cool. So, make sure you discuss them before playing. Sometimes, *littles* have difficulty saying what they mean, so Dommes, please make sure you ask and ask again.

> MOMMY'S_TOY: I've had difficulty figuring out what my hard limits are, let alone telling them to potential Doms. Mommy has helped me figure them out. She makes sure I am brave and tell my new Doms what they are.

The response posts continue, but I'm seriously going to make sure anybody I play with knows what my hard limits are. I've never been flogged or caned or whipped, so maybe these are soft limits. I've been spanked over Mistress Ciara's lap, which took a while to adjust to. I mean, I think I like it, but I'm not sure. I like pain, but maybe not a lot of pain? I won't know until I explore. And at the moment, I have no one to explore with.

I will allow myself one more post perusal before heating up a frozen pizza and then relaxing on the couch to a certain drink cart named Sarah, who I left getting fucked at both ends. But I'm pretty sure she doesn't mind.

The next topic is simply called *Power Exchange*. "Yes, yes, yes," I say out loud. "Tell me what this is." The first reply is from a guy. I think. Well, some lesbians like to be called Daddy, so maybe it's a woman. Who knows? *Kinks* is a strange, strange world, indeed.

COME_TO_DADDY: Power exchange is such an elusive idea to explain. There is Dominance, and there is submission. You can't have one without the other. The power a Daddy has is clear. He is the one who decides what happens to the sub and how her life goes. The sub's power comes in when allowing him to pull her strings and be the one in charge. She must allow this, or it cannot happen.

MIGHTY_BOI: I have a Mama, so SHE is the one in charge. It's not always Daddies who are in charge, you know.

COME_TO_DADDY: Yes, yes, you're right, Mighty_boi. But remember that some Daddies are women like me. There are all kinds of combinations of Bigs and *littles*, aren't there? Some Bigs want to be called Caregivers. Some *littles* aren't *littles*. They are *middles*. Thank you for the reminder. I will try to be more clear next time.

LIL_BIT: I think Power Exchange is a fantasy role play about the imbalance of power. If I use my safeword, then Daddy stops whatever she is doing to my body. I have power, too. If she didn't stop, that would be a true imbalance. I've heard that sometimes that's what men want—control over women to do whatever, whenever. If the sub has agreed to that, then yay. If not, then that's abuse.

MIGHTY_BOI: For Mama and me, a lot of Power Exchange happens during non-sexy times, like obeying her wishes and her commands while she's at work. In return, I trust her to keep me safe and protected. Always. Yep, I'm a Mama's boi. LOL

MOTHERS_WOODEN_SPOON: Well said, Lil_bit and Mighty_boi. Your Caregivers have nurtured you well. To me, Power Exchange has many facets, and one of them is sex. When play sessions are negotiated, both parties have needs. The Dominant and submissive explore their individual needs together. A sub may give over his/her decisions to the Dominant, but the sub has agreed to this. Like Lil_bit said, one utterance of a safeword takes that negotiated item away from the Dominant.

COME_TO_DADDY: Of course, and decisions about the sub's life don't have to be restricted to sex. I have taken control of other aspects of my *little's* life as well. Like what clothes she puts on in the morning, that is, *if* I allow her clothes.

MOTHERS_WOODEN_SPOON: Obviously, it varies depending on the dynamic. But I hope you're helping her learn how to make choices of her own, too. *Littles* need to grow—in their own time, of course. I encourage my baby girls to pursue meaningful careers and life paths. I help each of them on their journeys until they feel they've outgrown me, just like all children do.

I feel so sad for Mothers_Wooden_Spoon. It must be heart-breaking when babies leave the nest. That's precisely what Mistress Ciara said to me, "All baby birds must leave the nest sometime." But I didn't want to leave her nest. I'd just gotten there. And I don't want to have a Mommy Domme who will set me free. I want a Domme like Sarah's in the book. Who knows how to treat her subs and make them happy. Maybe a Mommy is *not* what I want.

With a disappointed sigh, I shut the lid to my laptop and head to the kitchen. I throw a frozen pizza into the oven and pace back and forth on the linoleum, but the pacing only agitates me further. An idea pops into my head. I get a towel from the linen closet and place it on the living room carpet. I imagine Sarah's Ma'am is here, and she has named me Six. She tells me to kneel. I do so on the towel to save my knees and sit back on my heels. I imagine she tells me to present, so I open my legs and place my palms face down on my thighs. "Palms up," she says to me. I turn my hands over. "Back straight and relaxed, please." I try to relax my muscles one at a time, the way Sarah did in the story last night. It's working. "Good girl," she says to me. My eyes are closed, so it is a surprise when she caresses my cheek with the back of her hand. "Hands behind your back now. Hold onto your wrists. Display your breasts to me, please." I do as she asks and feel the tickle of arousal between my legs. Sarah said her Ma'am conditioned her subs to become aroused at certain images. These poses are arousing, too.

All too soon, the timer rings, and my nutritious preservative-laden meal is ready. In a rare move, I sit at my tiny kitchen table to eat. For dessert, I will allow myself to check out all those Mommy Dommes pages, but for now, I prop up my phone and find Sarah in the story right where I left her.

Chapter 8

I Know You

I wake up before my alarm, bright-eyed and bushy-tailed. I laugh. Where the hell did that expression come from? Maybe from those people who are into pet play, literal pet play. You know, the ones that wear tails inserted into their backsides and imagine they are puppies or kitties or something? That hasn't ever been appealing to me, but maybe that might be considered a soft limit. You know, like, I don't think it's my thing, but if it's yours, then maybe I'd be willing to try. Maybe.

I pad to the kitchen nude and turn on the coffee pot. I tap my e-reader and start reading. I know, I know. My eyes aren't even open yet, and I'm reading erotica. This is my life now, I guess.

> Sarah was allowed a short break to freshen up after servicing the couch twins. During this time, her personal toys were thoroughly washed and sanitized by Three, including the nipple clips that had been removed. Bobbie had promised to pummel Sarah hard, and she did. The Dame also took her turn, and Sarah had three SRs total while they used her, but at no time did she let her voice be heard. The breathing techniques Ma'am had been teaching her worked. Bobbie was annoyed that she'd lost the bet to the Dame, but Sarah knew she'd pleased her Ma'am, and that's what mattered in the end. At some point, Ma'am had promised to teach her how to have a voiceless SR if all breathing holes were plugged. A dildo in the throat and fingers pinching the nostrils closed, something like that. Sarah was a bit nervous about that

65

training and hoped none of Ma'am's guests tried that on her before she was ready.

Once she'd used the restroom, cleaned up, and stretched a bit, she was ready to go back out. Three placed the drink cart on her back, secured it snugly, and then held the slave wing door open for Sarah to continue her path around the living room. Two restocked the cooler with fresh ice and drinks.

"Stop," said a commanding voice that wasn't Ma'am's. Sarah did as instructed. A dark-skinned hand grabbed her face and squeezed hard. It didn't hurt much, and Sarah knew not to expect bruises. "You have a beautifully sculpted body, Five," the voice said. Sarah wasn't entirely sure it was the hot, dark-skinned woman from the wing-back chair, but she hoped it was. Sarah's cheekbones pulsed with pain, and her breathing labored somewhat. "Do you like this, whore?" Sarah nodded as best she could in the clutches of the Domme.

"I am Mistress Flavia. I know you don't speak, but you may kiss my hand." She let go of her firm grip and presented the back of her hand to Sarah's lips. Sarah kissed her hand repeatedly. She didn't choke up, though, because only Ma'am brought up that emotion in her. "You will lick me for a little while, Five, before I heat up that backside of yours. Would you like that?"

This time, she nodded three times to let the mistress know she honestly did want that. Not that her wants mattered. It was all about Mistress Flavia's wants and needs.

Mistress tucked the bottom of her skirt up into her

waistband, revealing an unshaved yet trimmed pussy. Sarah stuck out her tongue, and Mistress Flavia maneuvered her body toward the tongue. Sarah salivated. This was another thing Ma'am had conditioned her and the other slaves to do.

Sarah didn't have much leeway in terms of movement, what with those drinks attached to her back and all, and she had no use of her hands to split Mistress's dark furrow, so she did the best that she could with her tongue. Sarah sighed contentedly. The mistress tasted like honey. No lie. Spiced honey or something, and Sarah lapped her up like she hadn't tasted pussy in years. Mistress Flavia's strong hands gripped the back of Sarah's head and smashed her face against her sex. It was harder to work that way, and Sarah had to find creative ways to get a breath, but she was doing fine. Ma'am did that kind of thing to them regularly, so it was sort of routine at this point. Sarah sucked the mistress's fleshy, swollen labia into her mouth like the business end of a vacuum cleaner and then thrust her tongue inside. Her nose smashed against the mistress's clit so that she couldn't get to it properly. Mistress Flavia had other ideas anyway. She undulated her hips against Sarah's face, rubbing her clit and pussy against Sarah's nose, lips, tongue, and chin. She seemed to like Sarah's chin the best, so Sarah steeled her jaw as the mistress rubbed her raw.

"Suck me," the mistress said as she released Sarah's head. Sarah lunged for her clit and sucked and licked for all she was worth. She made the tip of her tongue hard and gave the clit in front of her a beating. She wrapped her lips around it and sucked in short bursts. She circled the clit several times until a hand gripped the back of her head.

The mistress held Sarah's head more gently this time. Sarah knew what that meant; Mistress Flavia was close to orgasm.

Ma'am trained her slaves on many different women so they would recognize the various signs of impending orgasm and know how to please. Sarah wasn't very good at first, but Ma'am helped her become much more intuitive about each woman's pleasure. Pleasing guests was the most important thing in Sarah's life. Always. And she had to pay attention to every subtlety. And at that very moment, Mistress Flavia's pussy was Sarah's world.

"Good girl," Mistress Flavia said softly with a moan. She dragged her fingers through Sarah's hair, scratching Sarah's scalp. She undulated slightly, her breath coming in short gasps. She was almost there. Sarah sucked her clit rhythmically. The mistress's hand stilled on Sarah's head. Mistress's moans came from deep inside, and her pussy spasmed against Sarah's lips and chin. It was always the best moment for Sarah because it meant she had done a good job, and Ma'am would be pleased. Sarah kept up her ministrations until the mistress stepped back. With a satisfied sigh, she let her skirt down and grabbed Sarah's face again. "I can't wait to fuck that ass of yours, Five."

Sarah nodded and worked to catch her breath. She had to do it quickly because, clearly, Mistress Flavia wasn't done with her yet.

Resisting the urge to finger myself, I stand up and pour myself a cup of coffee. I don't have to be in until nine for the Elementary Functions final exam at ten, so I have plenty of time to read a bit more and have an SR of my own.

I put a couple of pop tarts in the toaster and head to my laptop. Oh, shoot, I never closed it down before going to bed.

Kinks is still up and running, and I have a message. Probably another dick offer. If I were into dicks this website would be a treasure trove. But I'm not into dicks. Unless they're strapped onto a Domme, then yes, indeed. I click open the message.

MAMA_LUVS: I know you.

My heart leaps into my chest at the first three words. Who is this? Holy fuck. How do they know who I am? I was careful. Wasn't I? That girl. I shouldn't have mentioned the stupid bracelet. Or maybe it was someone at the DIY store. I shouldn't have bought all those things at the same time. Anyone could see it was a cart filled with pervert kink gear. Oh. My. God.

The toaster pops, and I bolt out of my chair to get as far away from the laptop as I can. I try to get my breathing under control as I carefully place the pop tarts on a plate and rub at the instant headache that has started in my temples.

I have to read the rest of the message. I have to know what they know. Am I going to be blackmailed? I abandon the pop tarts, head back to the laptop, and sit down. My core is shaking.

> MAMA_LUVS: I know you. I've met many like you who are struggling to be Big but live in a *little's* mindset. Excuse me, a *middle's* mindset. Life can be challenging, can't it? Life can be overwhelming. I know. I'm a Mama Domme, and I know what you're feeling, dear heart. I know your predicament. Your journal posting was a thinly veiled cry for help, a cry for someone to help you understand the world around you.

> I don't know if I am the one for you, but know that I've helped *littles* before. My last one decided she wanted a Daddy Dom instead of a Mama Domme, after all. Disappointing as hell. Oh, sorry, Mamas sometimes use

69

naughty words like that. You, however, would not be allowed to just so we're clear.

Anyway, maybe we can talk for a bit and see if we're a fit. Does that sound all right, crystal_toy? If we are a good fit, know that vegetables before sweets is one of my mantras. Perhaps you can start that one today? Please wash behind your ears, and don't be late for work or school. Sincerely yours, Mama_Luvs.

I sit back. My jaw is open, slack with relief. She doesn't *know* know me. She isn't one of my students or anyone else I know personally. But she almost gave me a heart attack. "Holy shit," I say out loud, but then inhale sharply. Mama_Luvs would wash my mouth out with soap if she'd heard me cuss like that. And what's with this vegetables-before-sweets rule? I defiantly think about my cooling pop tarts and their sugary goodness. I wonder what her stance is on coffee. Hard limit there. You can control my orgasms but don't mess with my coffee. I chuckle as my blood pressure comes down several thousand notches.

I breathe a sigh of relief as I head to the kitchen to snarf down my pop tarts and get in a few more sips of coffee. With nary a vegetable in sight, I hit the couch with my phone. I decidedly decide to let Mama_Luvs's message marinate in the inbox until I get back from work. This time, I'm going to think before jumping in. This time, I'll have Lisa check out her profile page before I make a fool of myself again. That settled, I realize I have time to read a little bit more, shower, and then hit the road.

Where were we now? I take another sip of coffee to fuel myself. Oh, yes, Mistress Flavia isn't done with Sarah yet.

Cold lube dripped down Sarah's butt crack. Mistress Flavia's fingers were slippery as she worked the lube in between Sarah's cheeks. She inserted one finger and swirled it around, then two. Mistress Flavia pulled her fingers out and then back in. She did this several times until she pulled out completely. Something hard pushed at Sarah's tender hole and then slowly inserted. She could tell by the widening girth that it was one of the butt plugs from her personalized tray. Once it was in, she realized it was one of the smallest plugs. She could have taken more. Mistress Flavia must have known that otherwise, the bigger plugs wouldn't have been on the tray. But that didn't matter, though, did it? Mistress Flavia was in charge. Sarah understood her role. She was an object provided by Ma'am for guests to use in any manner they wanted.

Mistress Flavia's hands rubbed Sarah's ass almost tenderly for a moment, but then she grabbed two handfuls. She squeezed. The pain was good. Yes. Very good, and there would be more. She had no doubt. "She pinks up nicely," someone said behind Sarah. "That is a nice solid ass. Suitable for spanking." The hands went away, but Sarah was prepared for what came next. The sharp sting of Mistress Flavia's hand connecting with Sarah's ass caused her to inhale sharply. Then there was another and another. Mistress Flavia got into a beautiful rhythm, and Sarah was lost in the pain and the cadence. Way too soon, the Mistress stopped.

"Ahh," someone gushed, and Sarah knew something was about to change. She wasn't sure if she was about to get fucked or if Mistress Flavia was going to beat her with something else. The answer came quickly as a wooden paddle thwacked against Sarah's buttocks. The drinks in the cart clinked violently against each other, and it was Sarah's duty to make sure they didn't spill.

"Look how wet the little drink cart is," someone said. "It's running down her thighs. Look at that." There was a murmur of agreement from several voices. Apparently,

71

Mistress Flavia had gathered a crowd. "It is positively glorious how slick and aroused she is, isn't it?" That was the voice of the Dame. "I don't know how you train these girls, but I must know your secret," Bobbie said. She must have been talking to Ma'am. And that meant Ma'am was watching. A flush of pride swept through Sarah's body.

Sarah had no way of knowing when the next strike would come; the cooler strapped to her back inhibited her view, but she seamlessly absorbed the strikes. Ma'am conditioned her slaves to respond with arousal to both thuddy beatings and sharp stinging ones. She taught that any touch on a slave's body by a Domme was cause for arousal and celebration because a Dominant had chosen them; she had deemed them worthy. That had been ingrained into Sarah's soul every day.

Sarah's focus went back to Mistress Flavia, who had chosen her body to play with. Honored, Sarah would do her best to please her temporary Mistress. The paddle strikes increased in frequency and intensity. Sarah was grateful because there would be bruising now. She couldn't wait to see them blossom and bloom. The other slaves would ooh and ahh over them because a victory for one was a victory for all.

Sarah had other owners before Ma'am found her, and almost all of them made Sarah count paddle strikes. Ma'am never did. And the guests knew that because of the no-voice rule. Sarah liked not having to count because she wanted her focus on whoever was striking her. Staying ever-present, attentive, and grateful were important tenets to Ma'am.

Ma'am taught them that pain was not something to be endured, waiting for it to be over. Oh, no. Pain was something to be cherished and absorbed into their very souls. Dominants showed their affection by using them this way. For Sarah, the pain she received from Mistress Flavia had turned into pleasure almost immediately. Sarah's eyes were half-closed as she received her strokes, and once again, Mistress Flavia stopped too soon. Sarah's ass was on fire and pulsing like a beacon for all to witness, but she wanted more.

Fingers dug at the butt plug. It was removed slowly, only to be replaced by a dildo. Mistress Flavia slid it inside, filling Sarah. She then pulled it out and repeated the process as Sarah's tender ass pulsed. The pistoning ass dildo continued, but Sarah heard rustling noises behind her. She was a mass of sensation and simply could not make sense of the sounds. Suddenly and without warning, something plunged into her vagina. She exhaled loudly and found herself breathing erratically. She closed her mouth and slowed down her breathing as Mistress Flavia fucked both of her holes. Sarah's breathing became more regular at last as she focused on Mistress Flavia's rhythm.

Mistress Flavia bumped against Sarah's ass with every push keeping Sarah's pain ignited. A huge SR was building. Two more strokes were all it took. When the SR hit, Sarah's body froze and then jumped all on its own. She shook uncontrollably with every spasm. She barely registered the crowd applauding around her. Oh, they weren't praising her. They were congratulating Mistress Flavia's undeniable ability to bring out such a powerful response from a slave's body.

Mistress Flavia did not stop pounding Sarah, and soon, a second SR erupted from her body. Mistress Flavia's breathing got heavy, and the pounding increased until she moaned in orgasm. Sarah was so happy that her body had given Mistress Flavia pleasure, and she started to cry silently. "Aww, sweet little drink cart," someone said. "I'm going to have her next," another said in response. "Where's her toy tray? Are there nipple clips? Blindfold? Earplugs?" an enthusiastic third voice said. A fourth voice proclaimed good-naturedly, "Line up behind me, bitches." This caused the women surrounding her to chuckle.

Mistress Flavia finally pulled the dildos out of Sarah's body and sighed the most satisfied sigh Sarah had ever heard. The mistress came around in front of Sarah to grip her face again. She squeezed hard. "You're a lovely little fuck cart, Five. I am going to ask your Domme if you're on the market. She rarely parts with her girls. But rest assured, I will try."

The phone falls face down on my chest, and my fingers fly to my clit. I moan at the thought of women lining up wanting to fuck me, the slave named Six. I lift my pelvis as if inviting them to plunge into my body. My thighs open wider as if to give them access. A few more flicks, and I ignite. My body tightens, and I hold my breath until my orgasm rips through me, melting me to the core. My fingers keep stroking. A second mini orgasm flutters up, and I milk it out for all it is worth. I am about to pass out on the couch, but I can't. I have to go to work. I groan and set my bookmark.

"No," I cry in protest when the screen pops up, telling me this is the last page of the book, the end of the story. "No, no, no." I sit up and double-check. "Damn it. I want more stories about Five." With a frustrated sigh, I hit up the search engine and type in the author's name. There are no stories listed with the word Five in the title, but I see stories about One, Two, Three, and Four. How had I missed those the first time around? I purchase all four and then hug my phone to my chest. "So good," I say out loud and vow to remember to tell Lisa about this author, even though she probably already knows.

I leap off the couch and sprint to the shower. I have to get to work. Six has an erotica habit to pay for.

Chapter 9
Breathe, Breathe, Bernadette

I decide not to answer Mama_Luvs's message until after work on Wednesday because, on that day, I have a seven-thirty a.m. meeting with Dr. Wainwright and a ten a.m. Calculus One final to give. I can't have a distraction of that magnitude hovering over my life right now.

Tuesday morning's Elementary Functions final exam goes well, and I spend the afternoon grading in my office. I am so productive that I only have one box of exams to take home. On Tuesday evening, I am uber-productive and spend the rest of it ignoring *Kinks* and staying away from my new erotica novels. Talk about restraint.

I'm a little tired Wednesday morning and hope my commuter cup of coffee will make me sound coherent in front of Dr. Wainwright. I walk into the reception area of his office and find Miss Olga already sitting at her desk. I laugh and say, "Do you live here?"

Miss Olga winks and says, "He's always here early, so I am, too."

I take a shaky breath, and I know she sees how nervous I am. "Is he in?"

She nods and hits the intercom, "Your seven-thirty is here."

I bite down a smile because she referred to me as a number. If she only knew.

She gives me a quizzical look, but I ignore it and straighten up.

"Send her in," comes the response for the intercom.

"Good luck." She sweeps her hand toward the shut office door.

"Thanks," I mouth and let myself in.

"Ahh, Bernadette." He glances at me but doesn't get up or offer his hand. Something obviously important has his attention on the computer screen. "What can I do for you this morning?"

"I wanted to talk to you about my course load." I sit in one of the two overstuffed chairs on the other side of his desk. Oddly, his office is not large. Miss Olga's reception area is bigger than this.

He turns to face me finally. "You have two preps. Others have three."

Is the battle already lost? I look down at my hand. "Well, um, I know I'm the last hire, and that usually means you have to teach the courses no one else wants, but it's going on five years already."

"You're very good at what you do." He holds up a printout and finally looks up at me. I can't help but notice that his gray beard is neatly trimmed, and his button-down shirt is pressed with precise creases. He obviously cares about his appearance. He says, "You're one of the highest-rated instructors we have in the department. Your students say so in their evaluations."

"Oh?" I've never seen any of these evaluations before. I had no idea.

"Oh, yes." He puts the paper off to the side. "And your attendance record is perfect. I don't think you've taken a personal day since you've been here."

I shake my head. "I haven't. It's easier to be here."

"Bernadette, you're one of the strengths in our department. You've had great success where you are, and the students appreciate all you do for them."

"Thank you, Dr. Wainwright." I muster up as much courage as I can and add, "But I would like to delve into some of the upper-level courses. Graduate students. Group Theory. Rings. Commutative Algebra."

"I'm not sure anything's available. I'll keep a lookout for opportunities, but it's highly doubtful. Perhaps a summer course might become available at some point. I can't say." And with that, he adds, "Was there anything else?"

Guess not. Out loud, I say, "No. I need to get ready to give an exam."

"Good idea." He looks back to his computer screen, and I stand up. I have obviously been dismissed.

I plaster a fake smile on my face and open the door. Miss Olga looks up at me expectantly, and all I can do is lie with a thumbs up. She is on the phone and gives me a small wave goodbye. I am free to stew in my office until the exam. I sit with the lights off, trying desperately not to cry. Damn it! I blew my one chance. I was right there and couldn't make a case for myself. I just can't think on my feet, like ever, especially not when I'm in there with him. With a frustrated sigh, I get up and head to the restroom to make myself presentable.

~~~

At the close of the Calculus exam, my students trickle out, and I take pride in knowing that I have done everything in my power to get them to understand Calculus One. There were a few wandering eyes during the exam, but hopefully, I thwarted any cheating with a well-placed clearing of my throat and frequent walking of the rows.

Gratefully, one student stays behind to help me pack up. It's the Asian girl I saw at the grocery store who came to my office for Calculus help—the one with the bracelet that I should have ignored entirely.

She neatly, more neatly than I would have, stacks the exams inside boxes. I notice that she's rolled up her sleeves, and her BDSM triskelion bracelet dangles for all to see. Except there's no one else here but me. Is she deliberately flaunting it in front of me? If so, I'm not biting at it this time. No way. "Thanks for the help, Madison," I say to her. Earlier, when she handed in her exam, I snuck a peek at her name out of curiosity. I'm glad I did. Now, I don't feel so rude when I talk to her.

"No worries," she says. "I can use the physical work to calm my nerves."

"I'm sure you did fine on the exam." I pop the last box on the hand cart Miss Olga snagged for me from the janitor's closet.

"I hope so. I have to take Calc Two next semester, and then that's it for math for me. Thank goodness." She gets a stricken look in her eye when I chuckle. "No offense, Ma'am."

I roll my eyes. "None taken. I like math more than most."

She laughs and says, "I'll help you get these in your car."

"Oh, great." I wish I could ask her to come to my apartment building to help unload, but that will never happen in a million years.

"Ma'am?" she says as she holds the outside door open.

I clear my throat, wishing I hadn't. I keep signaling that calling me Ma'am means something to me. I hope she's not taking this the wrong way. "What's up?"

"My, uh, girlfriend reminded me to thank you for helping me."

"Oh, that's nice. Tell her it was my pleasure." Ooh, wrong choice of words.

"You know, umm, a bunch of friends of mine get together once a month for brunch at Rocco's. They have this private room in the back they let us use. Maybe you could join us one time. The first Saturday of every month at about ten in the morning."

"I …" I hesitate, not knowing what to say.

"I told Mistress–." She hesitates for a moment and then revises her words. "I told my girlfriend that it wasn't appropriate, you being my teacher and stuff, but she said, 'Madison, she won't be your teacher in January. And you're only extending a hand in friendship. That's all.'"

"She said that?"

"Mm hmm."

I wondered what kind of Domme she is to this girl. Is she a Mommy Domme? Obviously, I can't ask that. "She sounds wise."

"Oh, she is," Madison said emphatically. The softening of her face and body language tell me that Madison is very much in love with her Mistress.

"That's nice." I'm grateful when we finally reach my car. I unlock the hatchback. Together, we move the boxes in, and then she offers to follow me home and help move them into my "house." I don't tell her that I live in an apartment, but I do say, "Oh, not necessary. You've done way too much for me already. I have a neighbor's daughter who usually helps me with the heavy stuff, anyway." I wink at her. "She's an award-winning weightlifter."

"Oh, now that is a handy person to have as a neighbor."

"Absolutely." And it is an absolute lie, too. But she doesn't need to know that. I reach out to shake her hand because a hug is out of the question. "Thanks for the help, Madison."

"You're welcome." She turns to go but then says, "Think about Rocco's. First Saturday in January. Ten a.m."

"Okay," I say, but don't add anything else. I close the hatchback and hit the key fob to lock the car. I have to return the cart and beg out of lunch with Miss Olga and the others. I want to hit up a fast-food joint on the way home and then reread the message from Mama_Luvs and maybe, just maybe, draft a reply.

I finish up my third taco in the parking lot of my apartment building. The other six tacos will get eaten at some point, but I throw the bag of them in my briefcase for now. It will take me four trips up the stairs to bring all the boxes up. I honestly wish I had an actual weightlifting neighbor that could help, but then again, I don't. I don't want to get to know any of my neighbors. I don't want them to know who I am or what I do, mainly because I plan on moving out of this apartment complex the minute Jen is late with another rent check.

After forever, I finally get all the boxes up the stairs and situate them in a stack near my desk. I have five business days to get all of these marked, and the grades entered into the computer. I catch my breath and take a sip of Dr. Pepper. Somewhat refreshed, I head to the bedroom, take off my clothes, and toss them into the overflowing laundry hamper. Damn, I'm overdue for laundry. No worries, it's only down four flights to the basement and then four flights back up. Jen only has to go down two flights. Maybe she'll default on rent in January. Fingers crossed.

"Grrrr," I growl. There's no sense in thinking about Jen and my house right now. There's nothing I can do at the moment, anyway.

I stretch my overtaxed muscles and spend a moment using Five's technique for muscle relaxation. It works, it's so weird. I power up my laptop and make sure the little camera thingy is covered with a post-it note. I don't want any creeps spying on me. I sneak a peek at the eyehole in my front door. Yep, that's still covered, too.

Feeling safe and secure, I open up *Kinks.com* and re-read Mama_Luvs's message to me. "Wash behind my ears," I read out loud and chuckle. *Do I wash behind my ears?* I think I do. I'll have to pay attention next time I'm in the shower. And this whole veggies before sweets thing? What she doesn't know won't hurt her, right?

I feel a suitable response coming on, but decide to check out her page first. If that looks okay to me, then I will absolutely not trust my judgment at all. Lisa will have to weigh in, and if she says "no," then it's no.

I click on Mama_Luvs's name, which brings me to her page. Her profile picture is one of her peering down over a pair of mom glasses, you know, the kind with the chains on the sides. Her expression says she sees what you're doing, and you'd better stop it this instant, or there's a time-out in your future. It's a perfect mom picture.

She's probably in her late forties, and she seems physically fit. Not crazy fitness-chick fit, but she clearly takes care of herself. Is she pretty? Not exactly, but she is attractive. Handsome might be a good way to describe her. She isn't butch, though. I don't know. It's hard to describe her. Brown hair. Just above her shoulders in length.

I click open her other pics, but there aren't many. In one, she peers down at someone who is probably kneeling at her feet. Her expression is stern, and it excites me physically. In another pic, she's smiling and carrying a tray of lemonade. Oh, and there's one of her on a front porch. I love this one. She's snapping beans or hulling peas in a rocking chair, which makes my heart ache a little bit for my own mother. "Miss you, Mom," I say and look up. "You left us way too soon."

I take a big gulp of soda and can barely swallow against the lump that has built up. Somehow, I manage to get it down without choking. I'm not sure why that image made me emotional because I had never seen my mother snap beans or do anything like that. Maybe I'm pre-menstrual.

With a sigh, I skip back to her home page and read through her profile. There's nothing weird sending up red flags. Well, there's nothing strange that *I* can see. She simply states that she is a caregiver and wants to help her charges become strong and healthy individuals. Her hard limits seem to match up pretty well with mine, and she's into discipline. I laugh because what mom isn't? And, hey, I think I kind of like discipline, so maybe I should answer her back.

No, no, no. Lisa has to weigh in. I send her a quick message on *Kinks* asking her to check out Mama_Luvs's profile.

When Lisa doesn't get back to me right away, I am at a crossroads. Do I start reading *The Transformation of One* by E.J. Dubois, or do I grade exams? What would Mama_Luvs want me to do? Clearly, there is only one answer to that, so I push my laptop aside and open the last box of Elementary Functions exams. If I can polish these off, then I'll be two-fifths of the way through all my grading.

With occasional checks to the *Kinks* message board, I manage to plow through the rest of the box, enter my grades, and start on the Calculus exams. So far, most of my students are doing reasonably well, which completely gratifies me and validates my teaching methodology.

The red icon blinks above the message icon, and I drop everything to click on it. Yay, it's Lisa getting back to me.

RACHELS_TOY: Go slow with this one. Mama_Luvs seems okay to me, but always be careful. No sex in the first live chat, okay? I know you're busy with exams this week, but call me soon and let me know how things are going! I'm excited for you. Good luck!

I send her a quick note back, thanking her and letting her know that I will be in touch soon. And so, with all systems go, I push the exams aside and start typing a reply to Mama_Luvs.

CRYSTAL-TOY: Dear Mama_Luvs, Thank you for the nice note. I've recently discovered the label submissive to describe how I'd been feeling for many years, maybe even my entire life. My submissiveness has managed to clip my wings on more than one occasion, and I'm not sure how to change that. I'm not sure how to be strong and assertive when I need to be.

I think I would like to chat with you, Ma'am. I have perused your page, and I hope you will do the same to mine. This way, we'll have a basic understanding of each other if we decide to chat.

Sincerely yours, crystal.

I hit the send button, and the message goes off into cyberspace. Now, to do the impossible—wait for a reply. I stand up and pace the tiny living room. No, this will never do. I'm too wound up to go back to grading exams, so I decide to reward myself by reading *The Transformation of One*, which I've been chomping at the bit to start anyway. I set the timer on my phone for thirty minutes. I am not allowed to check my *Kinks* messages until that timer goes off.

I grab a bunch of towels for the couch and plop down with my phone. I really should use my tablet to read, but I'm already lying down. I scroll to chapter one.

Diandra hit the intercom. "Jade, please come to the playroom." Diandra waited five seconds and then hit the intercom again, "Now."

"Yes, Ma'am," came the breathless reply. "On my way."

Diandra sighed in frustration. It had been three months since Jade had come to live with her, and her sub remained scattered and unfocused, almost untrainable. But today, Diandra was going to try a new tactic.

"Kneel, please." Diandra pointed to the floor in front of her. The playroom in Diandra's isolated Victorian home took up a good portion of the second floor.

Jade kneeled in front of her Mistress and folded her arms across her chest.

"Proper pose, Jade. Please try to remember."

"Yes, Ma'am." Jade folded her arms behind her back and straightened up. She slowly lifted her eyes toward her Mistress.

Diandra had given Jade a spanking or flogging for her misbehavior, but she had come to realize that Jade liked impact, and these were not punishments for her at all. Diandra needed a new approach. "You didn't answer my page quickly, nor did you assume the proper submissive posture upon kneeling."

"No, Ma'am. I'm sorry, Ma'am."

"For these transgressions, you are to go stand in that

corner. Five minutes for each."

Jade looked toward the corner, confused. "The corner?"

"Go." Diandra kept her face neutral and her body relaxed. She didn't want her emotions to influence her new techniques. Diandra didn't move, and for the longest time, neither did Jade. Diandra tried not to grin, but she thought, oh honey, I definitely won't blink before you do. And then, much to her relief, Jade finally stood up and moved to the corner. Diandra followed her. "Keep this silver dollar coin pressed to the wall with your nose. Every time it drops, you get another two minutes added on." She handed Jade the coin and then turned to sit in her Queening chair to watch.

"Yes, Ma'am," Jade said with her eyes down. She placed the silver dollar against the wall and shimmied closer to pin it with her nose.

Diandra knew Jade felt her hard stare from behind. And that was the idea. This was a punishment, a true punishment, and it was about time Jade learned the difference.

I bookmark the story since it seems like a good spot for a break. And even though my phone alarm hadn't gone off, I couldn't take it anymore. As calmly as I could, I snuck over to my computer and lifted the lid. Oh, shit, there was a message. If it's from Mama_Luvs, then maybe this relationship will work. If it's a message from a creepy guy, then it won't. If it's from Lisa, then the jury is still out about whether it'll work or not.

I click open the folder. It's from her; it's from her. Mama_Luvs wrote me back. Breathe, breathe, Bernadette.

Chapter 10

Mama_Luvs

I get my breathing under control and pause before opening the message from Mama_Luvs. Is she the one? Will her message be the Christmas present I've always wanted?

"Oh, stop making this into more than it is, Bernadette," I say out loud. "It's a message from a stranger. Probably another whacko." I sigh, knowing that I might be right. Okay, fine. I will have no expectations this time. I get up and plug in my minuscule Christmas tree to set the mood and maybe bring me good luck.

I click open the message. It's long. Holy cow.

> MAMA LUVS: My dear Crystal, you say you are submissive. I imagine people tell you to "be strong" or "just do something." I know that's hard for you. A Mama Domme is someone who understands that and knows not to push you beyond what you're ready for. We are the ones who pull you in close and get the world to back off for a while.
>
> Submissives have two roles. One is to learn how to handle what life throws at them (and not hide behind their Dommes), and the second is to support their Dommes.
>
> Strong bonds, trust, and respect help them ground one another and help each other grow and flourish. I am all about personal growth.

I'd love to know more about you, Crystal. Are you still in school? Do you have a job or a career? Only share whatever you're comfortable sharing. I understand the need for privacy in this lifestyle. Do you have a family?

I have three children, all grown and launched. My ex-husband moved on to greener pastures (in his mind) a while ago. No grandchildren yet. I work at a desk job M-F, 7 am – 4 pm, and I live with a couple of cats. They're my watch cats. I'm being silly now.

That's the barest snapshot of me. If you'd like to pursue a friendship or maybe something more, message me back. If not, a polite message to that effect would be appreciated. Manners still matter.

Sincerely, Mama_Luvs

I am flushed with warmth. This message was different from the ones I got from Mistress Ciara and Goddess Julie. Mama_Luvs genuinely seems to want to know more about *me* and not just how to get off using me. No mention of sex, though. Maybe she wants a non-sexual relationship. She's obviously been in a heterosexual relationship, so she's probably not a lesbian. Maybe she's bi or one of those pansexuals who don't look at gender at all but the soul inside. That's a distinct possibility. Oh, wait, she said she had a girl sub before. Okay, so she's not new to this.

I reread the message and find no red flags. Well, Lisa might find a million, but I'm not going to show Lisa this message. There's nothing to show.

My stomach growls, and I need sustenance. Good thing I've got more tacos. I heat up three more in the oven, grab a Coke from the fridge, and sit back down to craft a suitable response.

CRYSTAL_TOY: I'm pleased that you got back to me so quickly. I am very mindful of a Domme's needs. I've only had one real Domme in the short time I've been out. She was strict and took care of my physical body (and I often took care of hers), but she wasn't very nurturing. After our one and only weekend visit, she tossed me to the curb. I know. That sounds dramatic, but I didn't see it coming (pardon the pun). She showed me a lot that weekend. She taught me that my body could endure a lot more than I thought it could. I was spanked that weekend for the first time in my life (except for a couple of childhood infractions long ago). I have never been flogged or paddled or lots of things. I'm very green, Mama_Luvs. I have some hard limits on the Kinks profile page, but I might have more. I just don't know.

And you're right about life being difficult sometimes, but I've managed. I guess what I want to say (quite awkwardly) is that I need someone to be tender with me and be careful with my heart.

Umm, to answer your other questions, I live alone (no watch cats), work 8 am – 4 pm, and have family on the west coast. I'm not sure what else you want or need to know.

Can I see a picture of your kitties? Thank you, and have a nice day, Crystal.

I could have been dirty and asked to see her pussies just to be funny, but she might think I'm a total slut. I send the message before I get bogged down overthinking and revising it. I always think too much. That might be half my problem in life. I wish I could just live. I need another taco and can't find one. Holy crap, I devoured all three while writing my response. I don't even remember eating them.

Knowing she probably won't get back to me for a while, I stand up, thinking I should go out for a walk or somehow get some exercise. Ah, but

One's story is waiting for me on my e-reader. I take my not-quite-finished Coke and head back to the couch. If I relieve some of the sexual tension I'm feeling at the moment, then perhaps I can think with a cooler head later if I get into a one-on-one conversation with Mama_Luvs.

"That's ten minutes," Diandra said. "Bring yourself and the coin here, please." Jade did as she was told and made her way past the king-size bed, the St. Andrew's cross, the spanking bench, and the various other equipment in the playroom. She handed the coin to her Mistress and then knelt in front of her. She put her hands behind her back in proper form. Her eyes were down.

"That's a good girl," Diandra said matter-of-factly. "You came right back here and presented yourself as I expected. You will be rewarded." This was part of Diandra's new approach with Jade. Rewards and punishments are based on behavior, both good and bad.

"Thank you, Ma'am," Jade said.

"Would you agree that Dom Martin didn't treat you very well?"

"Yes, Ma'am." Jade hesitated and then added, "I would agree." It was clear by her inflections that she did not want to speak ill of her former Master.

Diandra sighed and wondered how Jade could still be so submissive in her thinking about him. There were cigarette burns on her inner thighs, scars crisscrossing her breasts and torso, and deep white scars on her back from repeated abusive whipping. In fact, that's how Diandra came into possession of the woman kneeling before her. Dom Martin had been overzealous during a whipping scene at the local dungeon one night. He was playing it up to the crowd and completely missed Jade's safe sign. She had been gagged and blindfolded, but it was clear to everyone that she was in distress and was signaling that distress. He either didn't see it or, as popular theory had it, he ignored it. Either way, the management banned him from the club and asked Diandra to take Jade home for a couple of nights to care for her. Diandra agreed, thinking Jade would spend a night or two regrouping and then move on. But Jade was still there after three weeks. Although Mistress Diandra had no slaves of her own at the moment, it was well known in the community that she treated her slaves well and with dignity, and Jade knew it, too. So far, Mistress Diandra had used Jade as a service sub only. Discipline rituals had been put in place from the very first day. Slaves not only expect them but need them. Most craved them. Jade was no exception.

Thus far, Diandra had not used her new sub for physical pleasure, but that was about to change.

"The first thing I'm going to do is strip you of your name. The name Jade is from your old life. The one you had with Dom Martin." Jade looked up at her Mistress. "Since you are one of a kind, I'm going to call you 'One.' Do you understand?"

Calm seemed to come over the slave kneeling on the carpeted floor. She looked up and said, "Yes, Ma'am. Thank you."

"And now, since you've behaved well in these last few moments, I am going to reward you with a session. Please stand and disrobe." One did as she was told, folding her clothes neatly and placing them on a nearby chair. "You are no longer allowed to wear clothes while in my home, One. You may use a blanket in your bed at night, of course, but from now on, you are to be nude at all times. Do you understand?"

"Yes, Ma'am. I understand." One stood with her arms folded across her chest. She was clearly uncomfortable or unsure about where this turn of events would take her.

"Unless you have something in your hands when you're standing, you'll put your hands behind your back. I want those perky breasts thrust forward for all to see." One stood a little taller as she obeyed her Mistress. "And now, you can undress me."

One's face lit up. She carefully undressed her Mistress and stacked her clothes neatly on the other chair. "Go get me the first crop on the wall." One snagged the crop from its peg and handed it to her Mistress. She put her hands behind her back. Her eyes were down. "This will be your crop and yours only. No other slave will be disciplined with it. Just you, One. Do you understand?"

"Yes, Ma'am," One said. Her small smile was almost one of relief.

Diandra stroked One's face gently with the palm of her hand. It was a small gesture, but to a slave, it was a huge reward. "Thank you," Diandra said. Yet another reward.

Diandra stood to her full five-foot-eleven-inch height. She caressed One's breasts and nipples with the business end of the crop. "Beautiful breasts, One. You should be proud of them. You wear your scars well. They are unique to you." One nodded without looking up. Diandra closed the gap between their bodies. She lifted One's chin, forcing her to look at her new mistress. "You will always look at me when you speak or communicate. I must know that I have your full attention. This is not me being narcissistic. This is me training you to be an obedient slave." She stepped back. "Understood?"

One's eyes remained fixed on her Mistress. "Y-yes, Ma'am."

"Once we have finished communicating, then your eyes go back down, and you focus on the floor or your feet. Understood?"

"Yes, Ma'am." One lowered her eyes.

"Good. Good," Diandra said. Her crop continued its journey around One's body. Her feet, calves, thighs, back, and buttocks. The crop stopped inches from One's sex. She tapped One's inner thighs side to side. "You can trust me, One. I'm on a mission of exploration today. Spread those thighs for me. Let me examine you."

One spread her legs wider, and Diandra moved the crop higher. It came back wet. What had done it? The discipline in the corner? Being nude? Seeing her Mistress nude? The inspection? Maybe it was the affirmations and rewards when she'd done the right things. Perhaps it was a combination of all of those.

"You're aroused, One." It wasn't a question. "That is good. It means you will be ready for your Domme or one of my guests who wishes to use this part of your body. But for now, I want you on your back under my queening chair; your head toward the front, legs and feet out the back." The adjustable height queening chair was made of soft but durable faux leather that could be easily and thoroughly cleaned after use. Once One was situated underneath, Diandra sat on top, her sex split open and presented above her slave's mouth. "Service me, One," Diandra said simply.

One's warm tongue made a long initial sweep through Diandra's sex. Diandra moaned when the tongue flicked her clit. "That's a good girl," Diandra murmured. The tongue swirled around Diandra's opening and then plunged deep inside. One pulled the lips inside her mouth and sucked on them as if thirstily gathering nourishment. Her nose repeatedly bumped into Diandra's clit as she licked her Mistress. Lips replaced the nose, and One began a series of sucks and flicks and licks of different lengths and duration. Diandra looked at the slave below her doing her bidding, and her core tightened with power. It always did. The stirrings of orgasm built inside her. She leaned forward so her clit was more accessible. This also gave her access to One's head. She reached down and petted the head of the slave beneath her. It was a reward that One was being a good girl and that her new Mistress appreciated it. Diandra felt strong, invincible even.

The orgasm ripped through her like a flash fire. She bucked her hips against One's hardened tongue. "Good, good girl," Diandra moaned as she teased out the orgasm using One's tongue. "Very well done. You were born to service women." Diandra took a moment to catch her breath. "You followed instructions well, One. This pleases me."

Diandra stood up and retrieved the discarded crop. One still lay on the floor, not having been given instructions to move. Diandra tapped the crop into the palm of her other hand. "I need to warm up that ass of yours. And once your body is warmed up, I'm going to fuck you long and hard to see how you respond. Please stand to be inspected."

Diandra didn't have to run the crop through One's lower lips to see how aroused she was. The visual evidence was slick on One's thighs. "Did that arouse you, One? Servicing your Mistress?"

One looked up, "Oh, yes, Ma'am. Very much."

"Why?"

"Oh, uh, it's an honor to be able to touch you, Ma'am. And to please you in the manner that I did, to give you an orgasm, that is the highest praise, Ma'am."

"I see. And if I stopped everything right now and sent you to clean the kitchen, would you be disappointed?"

One looked down for a long moment, obviously reticent to answer. "Um, to be honest, yes, I would be disappointed." She looked up. "But not for the reason you might think. I do enjoy orgasms, Ma'am, but it is the fact that you would not be playing with me anymore that would upset me. That you wouldn't be finding enjoyment using my body."

"Mm hmm." That was an exciting revelation to Diandra.

"Ma'am?"

93

"Yes, One?"

"I feel honored and blessed that you kept me. I'm grateful." Her voice cracked with emotion on the last word. "Thank you."

"I see," Diandra said. "And I've changed my mind. I want you to clean this queening chair thoroughly." She pointed to the well-stocked cupboard with cleaning supplies. "And then you are to head to the kitchen and do the breakfast dishes. After that, please prepare lunch from the menu on the slave board. Remember, no clothes." She walked over to the two stacks of clothes and picked them up. "I'll take care of these."

"Yes, Ma'am," One said evenly, never once showing disappointment at the sudden turn of events.

Diandra headed into the hallway and murmured to herself, "And that's the last time you'll touch me in any way for the next two weeks."

"What?" I screech from where I lay on the couch. I feel betrayed. I'm horny as hell right now, and the Domme isn't going to play with her sub anymore? Of all the tricks to play on a reader. And what the hell is a Queening chair? I want to picture myself under it, servicing Mistress Ciara. Whoa! Where did that come from? I will imagine myself servicing someone, anyone, that is *not* Mistress Ciara. Mistress Ciara dumped me and does *not* get to be serviced in the fantasies going on in my mind.

I sit up and wonder what the hell is going on in Mistress Diandra's head in the book. She has a slave at her disposal. Why would you ban play for two weeks? And not just play, she banned all touch. That makes absolutely no sense. Mainly because I wouldn't last a day without an orgasm. Speaking of orgasms, I could finish myself off, but I decide not to. I'm going to stay aroused and unfulfilled just to see how One feels. What is it like to satisfy a Domme's needs but not your own?

Arousal spikes through me because I remember satisfying Mistress Ciara's needs, Mama Tatiana's, and Nik's without my own being satisfied. But then that wasn't true, now was it? Later on, they tripled teamed me. They filled every hole. Each one thrust in and out of me as they took my gangbang virginity. And Mistress Ciara took my ass virginity. My pussy pulsed at the memory. They collectively gave me the most earth-shattering orgasm I'd ever had and probably will ever have. I even passed out.

But what is it like to be used to satisfy others but never *be* satisfied yourself? That thought occupied my mind so thoroughly that I didn't remember getting up from the couch, pouring a glass of wine, and sitting at my desk. Mama_Luvs had responded. Oh, no. And here I am horny. I'd managed to do the exact opposite of what I'd planned. No, no, no. I'm not allowed to be satisfied, I tell myself sternly. It's not my place.

> MAMA_LUVS: It was nice to hear back from you, Crystal. It sounds like you had a professional Domme on your hands there – the one that "tossed you to the curb." I know those types. They use you to fulfill some kind of need they have, and unless you're going to become a paying customer, they discard you. Unfortunately, in the BDSM community, subs are known to discard Doms without warning, too. But I'm sorry that happened to you. I hope you are healing from it.
>
> And just so you know, I am in the USA in the Eastern time zone. Judging by your use of the words "West Coast" when describing your family, I would say that you are also in the USA but *not* on the West Coast. You don't have to tell me exactly where you are, but it would be nice to know what the time difference is between us because, as you know, little girls have bedtimes, so they will be rested enough to function well at their jobs.

I can't help the smile growing on my face. Mama_Luvs is mothering me already. Am I ready for this? Do I want a bedtime? And someone enforcing it? Someone meddling in my business? Well, I don't have to share everything with her, right? I read on.

> MAMA_LUVS: I would love to talk more with you, Crystal. See if there's a connection. If so, we can go for a trial period before committing fully. Too many people commit too soon. I don't collar my baby girls quickly just so you know.
>
> I'll be home by 4:30 pm today (Wednesday). Message me if you can chat then or later this evening.

I turn over my phone for the time. It's nearly 4:30 now. Do I want to chat with her? Yes, I do. Should I get Lisa involved? Damn, this is an angel/devil moment. Lisa might tell me to wait, but I don't want to wait. Lisa might find red flags in Mama_Luvs's messages. Lisa might make me block her. That last thought gives me pause. I don't want to block Mama_Luvs. I want to get to know more about her.

I hit the reply button and tell Mama_Luvs that I'm home puttering around and would love to chat with her. I say "puttering around" just in case I'm busy doing something and don't see her message come in. I have a little anxiety over that kind of thing since Mistress Ciara punished me if I was late to our chats.

I don't want to grade any more papers today, so instead, I look up Ohio eviction laws and procedures. The information I find is a bit cloudy and often contradictory, so I print out a bunch of stuff that might be useful. Once all my exams are graded, I'll make a concerted effort to sort it out. I hope that Jen is late with January's rent check.

> MAMA_LUVS: Crystal, are you online now?

CRYSTAL_TOY: Yes. And, just so you know, I'm also in the Eastern USA time zone.

MAMA_LUVS: Oh, great. That will make things easier. How was work today? My day was fine. Just like any other, except I need to get some Christmas shopping done.

CRYSTAL_TOY: Work was good. I have a ton of final exams to grade now. And my Christmas shopping is finished.

I cringe. Damn it. Within seconds, I gave her my occupation. I am a reasonably intelligent human being but not too bright sometimes. I vow not to give her my location. From now on, I will read over my messages twice before hitting send.

MAMA_LUVS: You're a teacher! That is wonderful, Crystal. It's one of the noblest professions. Working with children is a special calling. What grade do you teach?

Ahh, she doesn't know I am a university professor. Excellent. Does she think I'm an elementary school teacher? No, they don't have final exams, do they? Knowing myself, I will probably slip at some point and tell her that I teach Calculus. I know many twelfth graders in high school take Calculus, so that will now be me – a high school teacher. Now, I have to give her my first lie. Hmm, unless maybe I don't.

CRYSTAL_TOY: I teach Calculus. And the students are doing well on their exams so far. Fingers crossed.

MAMA_LUVS: Oh, you teach big kids. Good for you. And math. Wow, you must be a smarty-pants. I was fair at math but nothing earth-shattering.

CRYSTAL_TOY: You'd be surprised how much math you use in a day without realizing it. Estimations, proportions, probabilities. It's all math.
Mama_Luvs, may I ask you a question?

MAMA_LUVS: Of course. Oh, and if there's ever a question I ask you that you'd prefer not to answer, then say just that, okay? I value honesty above all things. Don't lie and make up something to fill the space. Go ahead now, ask your question.

CRYSTAL_TOY: Duly noted. Umm, I was reading a book today, and one of the scenes talked about a Queening chair. Do you know what that is and how it's used? (Remember how I said I was a newbie? LOL)

MAMA_LUVS: I'm laughing because of all the things you could have asked me, I would not have guessed that. Well, let's see. The seat in a Queening chair is basically u-shaped or an oval with a gap down the center. The sub slides underneath. Many are adjustable. At a lower height, I use mine for smothering my subs. Higher, you give the sub access to your princess parts for pussy worship. And, sometimes, a queening chair is used for water sports. Do you know what that is, Crystal?

CRYSTAL_TOY: Yes, I know what watersports are, and that is a hard limit for me.

MAMA_LUVS: Watersports are a hard limit. Noted.

CRYSTAL_TOY: What is smothering?

MAMA_LUVS: Smothering involves covering a sub's face so they can't breathe. Are you into smothering, crystal?

CRYSTAL_TOY: I don't think so, but I'm not sure about much of anything. There's so much I don't know. Why would anyone want to be smothered?

MAMA_LUVS: Smothering is exciting because of the inherent danger involved. The sub has to have immense trust in their Domme. And thank you for asking about something you didn't know. I never want you to fake your way through something. I will never judge you for your questions. Do you smoke, Crystal? I don't. Not anymore.

CRYSTAL_TOY: No, I don't smoke. And I only drink an occasional glass of wine.

MAMA_LUVS: Oh, I don't drink much either. Maybe a gin and tonic socially, but that's about it. So, what is this book you're reading?

CRYSTAL_TOY: It's called The Transformation of One by E.J. Dubois. It's about a Domme and her newly acquired sub. I've only just started it, but the Domme has an orgasm while in the Queening chair in one scene, from her sub underneath.

MAMA_LUVS: Male or female sub?

CRYSTAL_TOY: Female sub. Slave, actually.

MAMA_LUVS: I have never read this book. I'll check it out. Maybe we can read it together and talk about it. You can tell me how it makes you feel and ask me questions if you don't understand something. Like you did with the

Queening chair.

CRYSTAL_TOY: That would be awesome, Mama_Luvs.
I haven't read too far yet.

I chat with Mama_Luvs for another hour or so about nothing and everything. The conversation is smooth and feels good. And at no time did I make any more bonehead mistakes about my personal and private life. It felt like she was really listening to me and responding to what I said or asked. After a while, Mama-Luvs says it's time to wrap things up because she has to finish putting her dinner together.

MAMA_LUVS: It has been lovely getting to know you, Crystal. May I be brazen and bold and require something of you? This would be a small taste of what a Mama could do for you. I would like to establish a ten o'clock bedtime for you in which you send me a message on Kinks that you are powering down for the night and going to sleep. Now, I don't mean getting into the shower or brushing your teeth at ten. No, I mean IN BED at ten, lights turning off. Not reading your book at ten. All of that would have to be done by then. Good sleep helps little girls function well and think clearly. What do you think?

CRYSTAL_TOY: That's fair, I guess. I think I can do that.

MAMA_LUVS: No, don't think. Do. That's a Mama saying, btw. I'll look for that book and try to catch up. We can chat more tomorrow. Are you available tomorrow at 4:30 again?

CRYSTAL_TOY: I should be here. Grading exams or reading my book.

MAMA_LUVS: Or exercising. Or perhaps making a salad for your dinner.

CRYSTAL_TOY: Probably neither of those.

I pat my soft tummy, which has been getting softer and softer since living in the apartment. You'd think hiking up and down three flights of stairs every day would keep me in great shape, but alas, it hasn't.

MAMA_LUVS: Well, maybe we have a few things to work on then, don't we? I look forward to your 10 pm good night message later. And please tell me you will have a vegetable with your dinner tonight.

CRYSTAL_TOY: I will, indeed.

MAMA_LUVS: What a good girl you are, Crystal. Good for you! Okay, until 10 tonight. Mama out.

CRYSTAL_TOY: Crystal out, too!

I shake my head and blow out a sigh. I managed not to lie to her about anything. The three tacos I plan to devour in a little while have lettuce and tomatoes on them. Those count as vegetables, right?

Chapter 11
Merry Christmas, Mama_Luvs

Mama_Luvs and I have been chatting for two weeks now. I send her morning greetings, letting her know when I'm up. That's one of my new rules. And, I have to admit, I like the structure. Every morning she gets back to me, usually within an hour, and we discuss what my day will look like. She often makes suggestions about taking a walk or asking me how I am progressing with some task she's asked me to do, like putting a bowl of fruit out for easy access. But the conversations I like best are the after-dinner chats. She moved the 4:30 pm chat to 7:00 so she could get home from work, cook dinner, and then relax afterward with me in the evenings. It feels like she enjoys my company and wants to know who I am, unlike Jen, who barely seemed to hear a word I said during our last two years together.

Jen was probably thinking about Cassidy, her bff who she'd been cheating with. But I didn't know she was cheating. It didn't occur to me that she would do something like that. I guess our relationship had turned into an unspoken business arrangement—the kind where I supported her, and she did nothing. The only things we seemed to talk about were what needed fixing on the house or what she wanted to buy. Come to think of it, I was her cash cow, wasn't I? I have no idea how I didn't see it back then. See? Maybe I *do* need a Mommy.

But conversations with Mama_Luvs aren't like the ones I had with Jen. Sometimes Mama_Luvs and I chat and chat to 9:30 pm, and then she insists I get ready for bed, even though I don't want to. At 10:00, I send her my goodnight message. Sometimes she responds, sometimes not.

It's Christmas Eve, and I have no one to spend it with except Mama_Luvs. But that's okay because I *want* to spend this time with her. Every day, I think of a million things I want to tell her. Of course, when we're chatting, I can't remember most of them. Oh, well. We've even talked about sex, but mostly in the context of the book we're reading together. She sometimes asks me about the sex I had with Mistress Ciara and her friends, but it's almost an intellectual inquiry. I like that. Mama_Luvs has yet to discuss sex between the two of us, and I'm still not sure if that will ever happen. Maybe I should bring it up. Maybe next week. But that won't happen either because I am a big chicken.

I check the *Kinks* app on my phone and see that she's online now. I take off my sweats, bra, and panties. I debate leaving my socks on. Nah, I decide. Real slaves don't get to wear socks. I click open her message.

MAMA_LUVS: Happy Christmas Eve. How is my baby girl this evening?

CRYSTAL_TOY: Happy Christmas Eve to you, too, Mama_Luvs. I have a question about the book. Why did Mistress Diandra stop all human contact with her slave for two weeks?

MAMA_LUVS: Ha ha. You are not one for idle chit-chat, are you? Well, for one thing, like I've warned you about before, this book is a fantasy. It's not real. Oh, some aspects might be real, but it's a slave fantasy. It's kind of like the rape fantasy some women have, even though no woman I know would ever honestly want to be raped. Same thing with this book. No one wants to be a slave, Crystal. No one wants all their rights and their free will taken away. Even by the seemingly benevolent Mistress Diandra. Does that make sense?

CRYSTAL_TOY: Yes, it does. I mean, the word rape implies that it wasn't consensual, doesn't it?

MAMA_LUVS: It does.

CRYSTAL_TOY: Soooo … why does thinking about being a slave turn me on so much, Mama_Luvs? It makes no sense.

MAMA_LUVS: I think there are a few reasons some women have rape and sexual slave fantasies. Women are taught that sex is naughty and unladylike, that you're a slut or a whore if you like sex – which most of us do, btw. So, rape fantasies take the pressure off. Since you didn't initiate the sex, then you're not to blame. Keep in mind, though, that real rape isn't about sex at all.

CRYSTAL_TOY: It's not?

MAMA_LUVS: No! Not at all! It's about violence and power. Having control over someone without their consent.

CRYSTAL_TOY: Consent is everything.

MAMA_LUVS: Yes, it is. To be a sexual "slave," like One is in the story, means she isn't responsible for her actions. Mistress Diandra is. But that writer is doing a good job making us see Mistress Diandra in a good light. The mistress only wants what's best for her slave.

CRYSTAL_TOY: You're smart, Mama_Luvs. Did you say there were other reasons for people liking rape and slave fantasies?

MAMA_LUVS: Well, some people might be masochists and like it rough and like the pain caused by their suffering during the rape or the slave situation. If you were to act on these fantasies in real life, though, be one hundred percent certain that you can trust your partner. Otherwise, it could turn sideways fast.

CRYSTAL_TOY: Why did Mistress Diandra not allow One to touch or be touched for two weeks?

MAMA_LUVS: Right, right. That was your first question, wasn't it? I think she was trying to create a craving in One. A need for human contact so that when Mistress Diandra finally allowed One to kiss her feet, One was grateful and felt rewarded.

CRYSTAL_TOY: I get it. If I were denied human touch for that long, I'd go nuts. But then again, it's been about a month since another human has touched me. Sexually, I mean. And probably otherwise.

MAMA_LUVS: Since Mistress Ciara and her friends.

CRYSTAL_TOY: Yes.

Now would be the perfect time to ask Mama_Luvs about sex. But I can't do it. I'm too scared. I have to let her do it. Ahh, I am such a weenie. I really am.

MAMA_LUVS: Another reason Mistress Diandra denied human contact is because she wanted One to imprint on her. Mistress Diandra wanted to be the object of One's desires and yearnings.

CRYSTAL_TOY: Mama_Luvs? Will I ever get to meet you?

MAMA_LUVS: Actually, I've been thinking about that, Crystal. I live in the western part of New York State, so

I'm pretty far from the southern states if that's where you are.

CRYSTAL_TOY: Ohio.

MAMA_LUVS: Ahh, a buckeye, then?

CRYSTAL_TOY: Transplant, so not really.

MAMA_LUVS: Mm hmm. We could meet somewhere in the middle. I'll have to look on a map, but Ohio isn't too far from where I am. How about this? Since you don't go back to school until January, would you like to meet for New Year's? Spend a few days together, enjoying each other's company? Exploring each other mentally, emotionally, and, if you want – physically.

Yes! She mentioned sex! Yes, I want this. I think. Is it too soon? I would have to do the safeword and safe calls thing with Lisa and Miss Olga again. I can do that. Do I want to get physical with her so soon, though? We haven't even played online.

MAMA_LUVS: Judging by your sudden silence, I may have overstepped. We haven't officially committed to each other, and I know how hard it is to feel connected in a long-distance relationship. I have a thought on that, but before I go on, remind me of the rules we have in place for you.

CRYSTAL_TOY: Rules for Crystal are 1. Address you respectfully. 2. Morning greetings will be sent within 30 minutes upon waking. 3. Messages will be answered at the earliest opportunity, not longer than four hours, and all must be answered before bedtime. 4. Bedtime is 10:00 pm. 5. Fruits and veggies every day. And 6. Veggies always before sweets.

MAMA_LUVS: Ahh, yes. We haven't set up water intake or exercise routines yet. Those will be going in soon, sweetie, but for now, I'd like you to masturbate this evening.

CRYSTAL_TOY: You would?

MAMA_LUVS: Yes. Record yourself climaxing.

Holy shit! Did she just say she wants me to record myself orgasming? Oh. My. God. I've never done anything like that before. I reread the line. Yes, that's exactly what she wants.

CRYSTAL_TOY: Record it?

MAMA_LUVS: Yes. Use the audio recording app that comes with your phone. Or you can cover up the camera and take a video that will pick up the audio. It's about time I heard my baby girl cum. I want to listen to you cry out as you climax. You can send it to me at the email address I gave you. Do you know why I want you to do this?

CRYSTAL_TOY: No.

MAMA_LUVS: Because I want you to get used to cumming when you think of me. I want you to practice your release in a safe place without me physically being there. And then when I *am* with you, you'll be used to it. Now, I'm not going to give you instructions on *how* to pleasure yourself. You're a big girl and can figure that out on your own. But from now on, Crystal, I want a recording of your passion whenever you masturbate, even if it's fifteen times a day.

Holy crap. Can I do this? I don't even know what I sound like when I climax. Not really. I was trying to be like Five and cum quietly, but Mama_Luvs doesn't want that. Oh, my God, can I trust her? She's not given me any reason not to. Will she, like, sell my recordings? To the highest bidder or something? What would Lisa do? I'll have to send her a message and ask. But no. I think it's a harmless thing to ask for. And it's kind of turning me on that she wants that from me. And I'm taking too long to answer her real question. Damn it, why can't I think? Okay, okay, make a decision. It's just audio. No visual. She doesn't know my real name or anything about me. Decision made.

CRYSTAL_TOY: 15 orgasms in one day, Mama_Luvs? LOL. That sounds like a challenge.

MAMA_LUVS: Oh, it can be done. It can be done. But it's not a challenge for you, sweetie. And listen, I know what I'm asking is different. But you're not showing your face, and as long as you don't start spouting off math equations, no one will recognize your voice.

CRYSTAL_TOY: Okay, Mama_Luvs. I've never done this for anyone. It's a little scary for me. I want you to know that.

MAMA_LUVS: Only I will be hearing it. I promise. And hopefully, soon, I will hear it in person.

CRYSTAL_TOY: Mama_Luvs?

MAMA_LUVS: Yes, sweetie?

CRYSTAL_TOY: Will I get to hear your voice?

MAMA_LUVS: When we meet.

CRYSTAL_TOY: Okay.

MAMA_LUVS: Will you send me a recording this evening? As a present for me to open on Christmas Eve?

CRYSTAL_TOY: Yes, Ma'am. I will. As soon as we end our chat, I'll work on it.

MAMA_LUVS: You're a good girl, Crystal. A very good girl. And when you email me, describe the fantasy that went on in your head. What aroused you and made you cum? Tell me what toys you used or if you used your own fingers to rub your clit or penetrate yourself.

CRYSTAL_TOY: Mama_Luvs, you're arousing me.

MAMA_LUVS: That's because I'm appealing to your submissive side that likes to please. And this also pleases me. It's like Mistress Diandra in the story. She felt generous, allowing One to have the thing she most craved. And I am giving you what you crave. Sex. Sex that is indirectly linked to me. I will be on your mind as you touch yourself. I'm the one that wants the recording, so that will heighten your arousal.

She's right because I am thoroughly aroused and can't stop my right hand as it reaches down to finger my wetness lazily. My clit has become engorged by her words, but I don't tell her that. I don't tell her that I am touching myself. She may not like it.

MAMA_LUVS: I will leave it at that, baby girl. I'll expect your recording sometime before bedtime this evening.

I'm looking forward to hearing your voice, little one.

CRYSTAL_TOY: Okay, Mama_Luvs. Thank you for the task. I'll begin right away. Merry Christmas.

MAMA_LUVS: Mama_Luvs out.

CRYSTAL_TOY: Baby girl out.

My heart is pounding. I can't believe I agreed to record myself having an orgasm. My mind goes in a thousand different directions, none of them arousing. I take a deep breath and send Lisa a message. She gets back to me immediately and says it's no big deal and that she's done that for her wife many times. She told me not to say any actual words when I climax so no one will ever know it was me. She told me I would be fine. The funny thing is, I was hoping she'd talk me out of it.

I pick up my phone and find the audio app. I record myself saying hello a few times. I hate my voice in the recordings, but that's okay. I don't have to listen to it. Next, I pretend to climax and record the noises I make. I play it back and can't believe how much it arouses me further, but this arousal is laced with nerves.

I head to the bedroom and dig in my closet for my DIY stash. I pull out the rope, bandanas, and earplugs and toss them on the bed. I can't use the earplugs because I want to hear myself cum when I record it. And the rope, nah, I can't tie myself down because I need to manipulate the phone with one hand while the other is rubbing my clit. Bandanas? I bought them to gag myself, but I need my voice to be heard loud and clear, but yes, yes, yes, I can use them as wrist and ankle cuffs. I rip open the package and pull out four. I hastily tie one around each ankle and then each wrist. Nope, it's not tight enough. I redo them all. They're not the same as the leather cuffs Mistress Ciara made me wear, but still, they feel like ankle and wrist cuffs. Cuffs that a Domme would use to anchor me anywhere, force my legs wide open and spread-eagled on a bed or a cross. Oh, I wish I could gag myself. Should I blindfold myself? No, darn. I have to be able to see.

I realize the bag isn't empty and open it up again. Ahh, yes! The collar.

Yes, yes, yes. I put it around my neck and adjust it so I feel the weight, but it doesn't inhibit my breathing in any way. I snap the leather leash onto the D-ring in the front. After stashing the unused DIY stuff back in the closet under some shoes I never wear, I stand up and admire myself in the full-length mirror. The leash dangles lovingly down my torso and right over my clean-shaven princess parts. I laugh out loud. "Princess parts." That's what Mama_Luvs calls them. I reach for the leash and pull on it, imagining that my owner has it in her hand and wants me to follow her into the living room. She commands me to the couch, and I flop down on it. I register the tightness around my ankles and imagine she is binding my legs wide open. "Open those legs, slave," she says to me. "My guests are going to pummel that pussy tonight, Six." My arousal grows around this fantasy, and my breathing has quickened.

I tap open my e-reader to find out what joys Mistress Diandra has for One next.

> "Why are you on your hands and knees crawling, One?" Mistress Diandra held onto One's chin, forcing her to look up at her, not allowing her to avert her eyes.

> "I'm being punished for sounding like a 'cheap porn actress' when your guests used me this week. You said you never want to hear it again." One looked down, ashamed.

> "Correct," Diandra said. "I want genuine responses from you. That's what makes you one of *my* girls, not some cheap wanna-be." Diandra pushed her aside by her chin.

> One groveled and kissed her Mistress's feet over and over, her face wet with tears. "I'm so sorry. So sorry. I didn't mean to. Dom Martin made me do that for him."

> "Silence," Diandra roared. "I don't ever want to hear that toad's name again. From now on, you will be silent

unless spoken to. I only want to hear your voice if you have been asked a direct question. Is that understood?" The anger radiated from her like a tangible thing.

One looked up, eyes wide, and nodded.

"Nodding is acceptable. Preferable even." Diandra sat on a kitchen chair and gestured for One to settle between her knees. "Another guest is coming over this afternoon, and I expect to hear no sounds other than breathing from you. Is that understood?"

One nodded again.

"Good." Diandra pulled One's head between her legs and shoved her lace panties to one side. "You have about ten minutes to make me cum before the doorbell rings. And for your sake, I hope she's not early."

An hour later, One leaned back on her heels and licked her bottom lip. Mistress Diandra's guest was a stunning redhead, and her pussy tasted oh so sweet. Almost like pineapple.

The redhead tousled One's hair and said to Diandra, "She is gifted, Diandra. I haven't had an orgasm like that in, well, let's just say it's been a long time. One day, you'll tell me how you find these gems."

"One day," Mistress Diandra said from behind One.

"I appreciate being included in her training," the redhead said and stood up. The insides of her thighs were wet from her arousal and One's saliva. "What's next on today's training schedule?"

"Double penetration." Diandra had been working One on doubles for two weeks, and vocalizing during this process was what had gotten her into trouble. "We're also working on silence from her." She handed her guest a dual-purpose strap-on. One dildo was placed inside the bottom of the harness to be inserted into the user's pussy, while the second dildo stuck out straight ahead for insertion into One.

"Oh, Diandra," the redhead gushed. "You find the most interesting toys." She stepped into the harness and pulled it up her legs. "Insert that into my pussy, slave." One did as she was told. "Hold it there while I get the straps adjusted." One simply nodded and held the phallus inside. "This feels lovely. You can let go."

"Lay down on the bench for a moment, One," Diandra said. "Sex Doll, please."

One lay down on the wide leather bench and let her legs flop to the sides, her sex exposed to both women.

"Look how wet she is, Diandra," the redhead said. She moved in closer and stroked One's clit. "So erect." She looked back at Diandra. "All this just from pleasuring me with her mouth."

"She's being trained to become aroused by the sight of a woman's naked body. It causes a Pavlovian response, and she literally salivates from both ends." Diandra noticed the grateful look on One's face and gave her a private nod of acknowledgment. Rewards like that, no matter how small, went a long way when training a submissive.

Diandra slid four fingers into One's slick sex. The two index fingers and middle fingers went in back to back. She pushed the fingers away from each other, pulling One's canal wider. She then raked her fingers along the inside walls and out. She pushed One's labia away from the vagina, revealing the pink hidden inside.

"She is a beautiful young lady," the redhead gushed. "And I am amazed at how truly soaked she is."

Diandra nodded and repeated the movement with her fingers several times. "Flop over. Knees apart." Once One was situated, Diandra donned latex gloves and worked lube in and around One's smaller hole. She pushed two and then four fingers in and did the same widening technique.

"Look how calmly she takes that from you," the redhead said. "I can tell how much she trusts you, Diandra." Her voice became softer when she added, "And I can tell how much you value her. You've always been amazing at training slaves, but I think you've outdone yourself with this one. And, no, I'm not going to ask if you'd give her up. I know you won't."

Diandra simply smiled back at her guest and finished her manipulations. She carefully took off the gloves, wrapping them up inside each other, and placed them in the lidded trash can near the wall. She washed her hands in the sink and then instructed One to adjust the bench.

One nodded and pulled up one end of the bench so that one half was slightly elevated. Diandra donned a harness and lay down on the bench, dildo standing up rigid toward the ceiling. "Face me, One, and nestle my cock inside you," Diandra said softly. One nodded and flung a leg over her mistress and then lowered herself slowly. Diandra watched as the tip of the silicone cock touched her submissive's sex and disappeared inside. One knew enough not to move until one of the mistresses gave her further instructions.

Diandra reached inside the pocket of her vest and pulled out a chain. Attached to each end of the chain were clips. One's nipples were already hard but seemed to harden even more at the sight. Diandra clamped the first nipple, and One moaned audibly.

"Unacceptable," Diandra said. "I expect no sounds from you. You will be punished for that later. Do better."

One nodded and gasped when her Mistress attached the second clip to her other nipple.

"Much better," Diandra praised. "I knew you could do it." The praise was genuine, with no hint of sarcasm. A reward for a good response. "Lean forward."

One leaned forward, her hands on the bench above her Mistress's head, holding herself up. Diandra grabbed One's hips and thrust in and out slowly.

One exhaled breathily but did not use her voice. That made Diandra grin. Diandra increased the pace and then slammed the dildo into her submissive three times, driven to the hilt. One's mouth was wide open; her body shook as the sensations washed over her. But she was silent.

Diandra reached down and pulled One's ass cheeks apart. "In you go," Diandra said to the redhead, who had already lubed up the dildo in her harness. It was smaller than the one currently filling One's vagina.

"A treat, for sure," the redhead said and swirled the tip of the dildo against the puckered hole. She applied slight but constant pressure. The tight ring of muscles finally gave way, and she pushed in slightly, about an inch. She pulled all the way out and then pushed in again, this time gaining two inches. She continued in this manner until she was all the way in.

One's breathing had become hard and uneven. Diandra felt great pride in her submissive because, at this point before, One would falsely cry out in ecstasy, trying to please Diandra's guests. It was something Diandra always hated about porn. She firmly decided that One would watch her training porn with the sound off from now on.

Diandra thrust her dildo in time with her guest's. And it wasn't long before One's body started shaking. Her head bobbed from side to side, and her eyes rolled in the back of her head as the sensations overcame her. It was obvious she was having her first-ever *silent* SR. She slumped over, her SR finished, and it looked like she was having trouble holding herself up. Diandra gave her guest the high sign to pull out.

Diandra then pulled One down on top of her and hugged her tightly. "Good girl. Such a good good girl. You had a beautiful response to our stimulus, didn't you? A beautiful SR?"

One lifted her head and nodded. She mouthed soundlessly, "Thank you."

"Make sure you thank our guest, too."

One turned to face the redhead and said out loud, "Thank you, Mistress."

The redhead smiled and cupped One's chin. "You're a keeper, you are." She looked over at Diandra and asked, "May I?"

"Yes, indeed."

The redhead reached over to One's right nipple and undid the clip. One gasped voicelessly. The redhead tapped One's tender nipple, making her slump forward from the pain.

My own breathing is ragged as I lay on the couch, wanting to feel the same delicious sensations that One is experiencing. I'm so turned on right now but having second thoughts about recording my passion. Damn, why didn't Lisa talk me out of it? I place my phone on the floor face down and close my eyes, unsure what to do.

Chapter 12
Alone

Should I record myself? That second night at Mistress Ciara's, Nik said my orgasm was the best he'd ever heard. Arousal hits me hard, and it's decided. I'm going to record it. I'll decide later if I'm going to send it. For now, I'm still in control. That settled, I pick up the phone and make sure the app is open and ready to record. I place the phone on my bare chest above my breasts, where I can get to it quickly. I pull two clothespins from the bag with a shaky hand. My fingers caress my sensitive nipples, and I squirm with heightened arousal. I pinch one nipple tight and lift my breast by this singular point. I let go, and it bounces back in place. I snap a clothespin on the abused nipple and groan out loud. I would be in big trouble with Mistress Diandra right now, that's for sure, but I can see why One couldn't help crying out. It hurts. Especially right at first. But then the pain radiates and becomes something else. Something pleasurable. The second clothespin elicits the same response, and my legs separate on their own. I bend my knees and let them relax to the side as if commanded by Mistress Diandra.

I flick the clothespins and moan at the sharpness. I run both hands down my torso to my thighs. For some reason, I'm surprised that my skin is both smooth and warm to the touch. I am not surprised that my inner thighs are wet, though. I run three fingers over my smooth mons and into my wetness. I dip a finger into my well and trail the wetness up and over my clit. Slow and steady circles have my hips bucking lightly. I don't have a dildo handy. Dang it. Mama_Luvs mentioned fingers, so I forgot about dildos. I picture Mistress Diandra telling me to put her cock inside me, so I push two fingers inside my slick hole. The friction caused by jamming my fingers in and out is fantastic. I ram them in three times fast and hold them after the last one. I use the palm of my hand to rub my clit and moan at the sweet sensations. In my head,

Mistress Diandra morphs into Mama_Luvs. Her fingers are inside me, touching me, claiming me.

I sneak my other hand lower and then plunge two more fingers in. I rake both sets of fingers along my walls and out, just like in the book. I'm pulling the lips out, opening myself for Mama_Luvs. I can't see it, but I know my pink is swollen and ready. I flay myself open a few more times and then plunge back in with three fingers of my left hand. My right middle finger strokes my clit in time, with the other hand pistoning inside me. I moan as a sweet spark ignites deep inside. I moan again and remember.

"Shit." I have to record myself for Mama_Luvs. With a dry finger, I tap the record button.

I imagine a tongue circling my clit. Fingers plunge faster, and I moan in time with each pass around my clit. I inhale sharply and exhale the word "Ohhhhh." I slow my movements as passion fills my belly. It radiates outward, spreading, and melting every cell in my body. Then it rushes back to my sex, and I climax, hips bucking, moans reaching soprano in pitch. My body jerks as passion soaks both hands. I ride it for as long as I can and moan, "mmm, mmm, mmm." I come down breathlessly until I finally sigh and reach the ground again. I almost let myself doze but then remember the recording. I open my eyes long enough to tap the off button and then let myself fall asleep.

~~~

I shiver awake and sit bolt upright. I'm supposed to be doing something. I can't remember what it is. I'm cold. It's the last week of December, and I'm sleeping naked on the couch. No wonder I'm cold. I shrug on my discarded sweats. What time is it anyway? I find my phone deep in the cushions of the couch, remembering the powerful orgasm that knocked me out. But then my eyes shoot wide open. The recording. Oh. My. God. What have I done?

"It's okay. It's okay," I console myself. "You haven't sent it yet." And, besides, if I do send it, it's only 9:00. I have an hour before bedtime. I carefully place the phone near my computer and tread off to the bathroom. I've caught a chill while dozing on the couch in the nude in the middle of winter. Only a hot shower will cure this kind of chill. I can't think when I'm cold, and I need to think. I desperately need to think.

I turn on the spray and shiver on the cold tile until it's warm enough to go in. The hot water cascades over my head and body as I think about my next move. Do I send the recording? Or do I make some excuse? I could say Jen had an emergency at the house, or my brother called about Dad.

I wash my body and wash behind my ears. And then I laugh. So, it's true – I actually do wash behind my ears. Laughing makes me calmer and helps clear my head a little. I decide that I'm scared. This is something new that I've never done before. And I shouldn't start lying to Mama_Luvs now. First of all, she'll know that I'm lying, and honesty is one of her basic tenets—honesty above all else. If I lie, then we might be over before we've even started. I mean, come on, it's just a recording. With Mistress Ciara, I drove to Columbus and let her chain me to her living room floor. This is nothing compared to that.

I turn off the shower, wrap up in my softest towel, and hurry into the bedroom to don clean sweats and socks.

"The first thing to do is listen to it, dork. Then decide if anyone can tell it's you." I do love talking to myself. I make so much sense sometimes.

Back in the living room, I pick up my phone and find the recording. I tap the playback button and close my eyes. As I listen, warm heat rises from my chest and inflames my face. I can't believe I've done this. I am not an exhibitionist and this reeks of it. I take a deep breath and listen again.

On the recording, I hear my breathing labor, my moans grow, and my passion rise. I hear the climax loud and clear and relive it viscerally. Arousal spikes my body at the memory. I hear my breathing slow, and then the recording is over.

"Fuck, that was hot," I say out loud. I can't believe listening to it got me wet again. No wonder Mama_Luvs wants a recording.

I flip open my laptop and write up the fantasy going through my head as I touched myself. Mama_Luvs wanted details, so I tell her about Mistress Diandra's cock. I then tell her how the cock became Mama_Luvs's fingers and how she wanted me to be a good girl and cum for her loud so she could hear it in New York. Okay, so some of the write-up was improvised, but still, it was close enough to the truth. I send the recording to my computer and then attach it to the email. I pause before hitting send but throw caution to the wind and click the button.

I close the laptop, hoping I haven't just ruined my life.

I am meticulous and laser-focused as I get ready for bed. Teeth are brushed and flossed. Vitamins are taken with plenty of water. I get into bed and pull the covers up. I clutch my Pooh bear for comfort and tap open the *Kinks* app. There's a message from her. Dread settles over me as I open it.

> MAMA_LUVS: Hot, hot, hot! That was so hot, baby girl. OMG. So sexy! I wish I had been there to hear it for myself!

I groan in relief and let myself relax. I also melt because she called me baby girl again. I don't know what to say to her. I'm kind of embarrassed and feel exposed. A big part of me is appalled that I sent her a recording of something so intimate. I almost feel dirty.

> MAMA_LUVS: Your description was lovely, too. You did such a good job explaining your fantasy. Good girl. I am very impressed.

> CRYSTAL_TOY: Thanks, Mama_Luvs

> MAMA_LUVS: I can tell you're a little embarrassed, sweetie. Don't be. Sex is the most natural thing in the world, and I'm honored that you shared it with me. Now, don't worry. No one else will hear this. Let's make plans to meet. Can we ring in the new year together? Meet on New Year's Eve, stay two nights? Somewhere halfway between the two of us?

> CRYSTAL_TOY: I'll have to check my schedule.

> MAMA_LUVS: No need to be apprehensive, baby girl. It'll be just me. We won't do anything you don't want to do. Okay?

CRYSTAL_TOY: Okay, I'll let you know.

MAMA_LUVS: That's all I can ask. Are you in bed?

CRYSTAL_TOY: Yes, Ma'am. I am washed, toothed, and vitamined.

MAMA_LUVS: You're so cute. Here's what I want from you right now. Get out of bed, take off those pajamas. I want you to sleep in the nude from now on. I sleep nude. It's natural. I want you used to being nude 24/7 by the time we meet. Unless we go out, you will be naked in my company.

CRYSTAL_TOY: Okay. Yes, Ma'am.

MAMA_LUVS: And tomorrow, you will drink half of your weight (in ounces) of water. You'll do this every day. And you will exercise for a minimum of twenty minutes. I walk twice a day for at least an hour each time. You will need to be able to keep up with me when we meet.

CRYSTAL_TOY: Yes, Mama_Luvs. I understand. Water and walking. Got it. P.S. The PJs are off. I am in my birthday suit.

MAMA_LUVS: Back in bed?

CRYSTAL_TOY: Yes, Ma'am.

MAMA_LUVS: No touching yourself tonight. No vibrators.

CRYSTAL_TOY: I don't have a vibrator.

MAMA_LUVS: ???

CRYSTAL_TOY: I used to have one. But when I was with Jen, it was hard to sneak off and masturbate with a vibrator. I mean, she was *always* home, and the vibrator was loud, so I never used it. I threw it out.

MAMA_LUVS: We do what we need to do to survive, don't we? Well, little one, you need your sleep.

CRYSTAL_TOY: I am kind of tired.

MAMA_LUVS: Masturbating wore you out, dear. If you play with yourself tomorrow, you will send me a recording and a write-up of your fantasy. I think I want one from you every day. Let's make that so, shall we? At least one new recording every day. As for me, I'm going to go read about Mistress Diandra and One. You made it sound so sexy. Goodnight, baby girl. Mama_Luvs out.

CRYSTAL_TOY: Oh, okay, bye. Crystal out.

And that was that. A bunch of new rules, and she's left me alone again. Sometimes, she leaves so abruptly, without a proper goodnight. It's like I've been dismissed. I have, haven't I? There were things I wanted to talk to her about, though. Like how making the recording made me uneasy. But she led the whole exchange. I guess that's what dominants do. Lead. I'm just the submissive. My role, duh, is to do what she tells me to do and to please her. Apparently, water, walking, and recordings of masturbating please her. And those I can do.

~~~

During the next week, Mama_Luvs and I settle on meeting in

Marquestown, Ohio, for our New Year's Eve rendezvous, which is *tomorrow!* I try not to hyperventilate as I stand here naked, ironing the clothes I'll be packing and wearing. I'm even ironing the pajamas, AKA sweats, she told me to bring. I've already cleaned my car inside and out, just in case she wants me to drive us around.

When we were settling on a location, I lied and said Marquestown was only three hours away, but it's technically four. I don't want her to know exactly where I live. I've already given up too much by telling her I live in Ohio. But she would know that as soon as I pulled up since I have Ohio plates. Oh, shit. Can she trace who I am by my license plate? Hopefully, that's not an easy thing to do. Or maybe the VIN number? I'll have to make sure I cover that or something. Maybe mud on the license plate?

"Hello, paranoia," I say as I put the finishing touches on the shirt I'll wear tomorrow in the car. I can't go on my trip in a distrustful state of mind. I have to trust. With Mistress Ciara, we met at a restaurant first, and then she sent me home. That gave me time to process who she was and if I wanted more with her. But with Mama_Luvs, whose real name I don't even know, I'm going right to the hotel room. She'll probably have me strip naked immediately.

I finish ironing and packing and get dressed to head out for my second walk of the day. I have to be able to keep up with her. I don't want any punishments because I have no idea if she's a sadist or what. And if she is a sadist, how far will she go? Hopefully, as far as my safeword allows.

I plunk a knit cap on my head and wooly gloves on my hands and head out for my walk. The route I take out of the apartment complex puts me on a busy two-lane road that people use as a cut-through between two main roads. I don't mind because the sidewalks are wide here and there are a lot of trees. It makes me forget that I live in the outskirts of a midwestern city. The air is cold in my lungs, but I don't mind. It helps clear my head.

I nod and say hello to the young woman walking a very well-behaved Labrador. I've seen her every day on my evening walks, and she always says hello to me and makes eye contact. The dog walks at her heel and looks up at her as if waiting for his Mistress's command. Is that what Mama_Luvs is doing to me? Training me? Am I waiting to follow her every command?

Is she trying to get me physically fit so I will be healthy and strong

124

enough for her to use and abuse? I mean, exercising like this and eating healthy are good for me, of course, so I don't mind. But I'm not allowed to masturbate or even touch myself today or tomorrow. I think it's because she wants me yearning for her when we meet.

Tomorrow morning, I will be shaving to be fresh and clean for her, but I will not be touching myself beyond that. And I have to do a good job. She said there would be a punishment if I present myself to her in a sloppy or wrinkled condition. That's why the iron came out, and all the clothes are pressed.

I check my watch and find that I have reached the fifteen-minute mark. I spin on my heels and hustle home. It's just too darn cold to stay out here any longer than thirty minutes total. Besides, I have to call Lisa and then Miss Olga to make sure they can be my safe-call people.

Once inside, I strip and then chug a 16-ounce bottle of water. I'm floating away with the amount of water she has me drinking. I'm getting cold, and since I'm not allowed to masturbate to warm up, I make a cup of decaf green tea to sip while I call Miss Olga and set her up as one of my safe calls. Since it's decaf, Mama_Luvs said the tea counts in my total number of daily ounces. Miss Olga finally answers her phone and heartily agrees to help me out. We chit-chat for a few moments, but she doesn't mention my spring schedule at the university, and neither do I. I got the official email yesterday: same courses, same course load. As I suspected, my meeting with Dr. Wainwright was ineffective. He isn't ever going to give me better courses to teach. I'm just a pawn, not to be taken seriously, and I have to face that. I wish I could talk this over with Mama_Luvs, but I don't want her to know I'm a university professor. She thinks I teach in a high school or something.

I make a second cup of tea to increase my water intake and text Lisa to call me ASAP. I laugh when the phone rings in less than a minute. This time I think our roles are switched. This time, *she* is the one who is excited and gung-ho about me traveling out to meet a dominant, and it is me who's apprehensive and hesitant. Lisa says I'm nervous because maybe Mama_Luvs is "the one." I scoff at that and tell her that I have no expectations this time and I'm not rushing into anything.

Lisa heartily agrees to be one of my safe-call people, and we go over the timing of my texts and our secret code words. She makes me promise not to make a list of the code words in my phone, you know, just in case someone else figures out what I'm doing. That spikes my nerve center, but she laughs at me and tells me to chill out, that I'll be okay. There are lots of people at a hotel, she reminds me. Many of them with ears. I burst out laughing and wish she could see my eyes rolling!

"Hey, B," Lisa asks, "I'm on the hotel's website, and I think it has a restaurant."

"Uh, yeah, there is. Why?"

"Meet her there. Don't go up to the hotel room first thing."

"Ahh," I say. "That's a great idea."

"Yeah, that'll give you a little while to suss out who she is and if you want to spend two whole nights with her."

"Yeah, yeah, that makes sense. You're a genius, my friend." I sit back in my desk chair, feeling my body relax with relief. Yes, that *is* an excellent idea.

"And this way, if she creeps you out or whatever, you can get right back in your car and drive home."

"That makes sense."

"All right, I should get going. Don't forget to send a text when you leave tomorrow," Lisa says.

"I won't forget."

"And good luck sleeping tonight. Too bad you can't do any self-care to get you sleepy."

"I wish," I say with a laugh. "Goodnight, friend. Take care. Sleep well."

We hang up after a few more exchanges, and then I am alone again. My tea is gone, but it and the conversations with Miss Olga and my good friend Lisa have warmed me considerably. Maybe I'm not as alone as I think.

I get up and sigh. The only thing to do now is double check my suitcase, make sure I have enough cash, and go to bed. Alone.

Chapter 13
Happy Little Slave

I make good time as I drive northeast on I-71 toward Marquestown. The ironic thing is that I have to go right through Columbus, Mistress Ciara's hometown. I briefly consider getting off the highway and driving by her townhouse but decide against it. That ship sailed. And besides, I'm not the stalker type.

When I got up this morning, I freshly shaved everything and made sure the clothes I put on were still neat and tidy. My GPS said the trip would take about four hours and fifteen minutes, so I left early to allow 5 hours. When I'm three hours away from our agreed-upon meeting time, I'll send Mama_Luvs a message on *Kinks* that I'm on my way. I already texted Lisa, and she texted me back immediately, wishing me luck and reminding me of my safe call times and code words.

The lease on my morning coffee expires abruptly, so I pull off the highway, find a Hungry Hamlet's, and use the facilities. I shouldn't, but I decide to get a breakfast meal to go. To redeem myself, I ask for bottled water instead of coffee. I'll ditch the fast-food bag somewhere along the way so Mama_Luvs doesn't see it and pitch a fit.

The one thing I don't want is a repeat of the Mistress Ciara thing. "You can't go all sub-frenzy this time," I say out loud. It helps to remember something difficult by saying it out loud. That way, you're using another modality to solidify the concepts in your brain. I look at my reflection in the rear-view mirror and say, "I mean it. No sub-frenzy!" I nod in agreement. Calm and cool. That's me. Uh huh, sure.

When I pull into the hotel parking lot, my heart is pounding. I'm right on time, and know Mama_Luvs is here already. She messaged me to tell me that she's inside the hotel restaurant. The hotel is nice. It looks just like the pictures on the website. Thank goodness this isn't some rundown, seedy motel. I text Lisa that I made it to the hotel and that I will text her again later at our agreed-upon time. I also text Miss Olga to let her know I made it to the hotel. She sends me a good luck message and, like Lisa, tells me to have fun. Here's hoping.

I take a deep breath and get out of the car. Before closing the door, I practice breathing while checking my pockets for my wallet, keys, and phone. Those things verified, there's nothing left for me to do but head in. It's cold out here anyway. I take a step toward the hotel lobby and say, "Here goes nothing." I'm shivering as I walk up, and it is not just from the late December cold, this I know for sure. I purposely left my bag in the car so I would have to go back out and get it. I know myself. I am going to need a moment to calm my nerves later.

The doors to the lobby woosh open, and I am trying to look calm as I search for the restaurant. It's not immediately obvious, dang it. Oh, wait. There's a small sign that says "Rust Belt Grille" with an arrow pointing left. I head down the long, lonely corridor and find the practically empty restaurant. I notice the white tablecloths first. Uh, oh. Is this a high-end restaurant? The wait staff are wearing black pants and white button-down shirts with black ties and black aprons tied around their waists. This place is fancy. There are businessmen having coffee in front of the large windows in the back. There is only one other patron in the place. Sitting at a table overlooking the courtyard is a woman sitting alone. She's absentmindedly stirring her coffee. I feel empowered for some reason because I've seen Mama_Luvs before she's seen me. She looks just like her pictures on *Kinks*. She is fit, and her dark brown hair has only a little bit of gray in it, but it makes her look distinguished somehow. Her sweater is kind of mom-ish, and she has eyeglasses hanging around her neck on a cord, but she is not old-looking. She is lovely.

She looks up and smiles when she sees me. She must have felt my presence. My own smile grows, which I can't help. I wave, and even though my nerves are buzzing in my core, I try to look at ease as I head toward her.

"Crystal!" She gets to her feet and wraps me in a hug. I have no choice but to put my arms around her and hug her back. She lets go and says, "You're so pretty." Before I can react, she says, "How was your trip? Take your coat off. Stay awhile."

I chuckle and do as I'm told. "It's nice to meet you finally." I sit across from her at the table.

She is positively beaming at me. "You are so cute, little girl. Look at those dimples." I feel the warmth radiating from my face and hope no one overheard her call me that. She doesn't seem to notice my embarrassment and says, "Your trip was good? Not too long?"

"No, not too long," I lied. "It was fine." I thank the heavens when the server comes by. I order a coffee. "And how was *your* trip?"

"A little less than three hours. Pretty doable." She reaches across the table and runs gentle fingers down my cheek. It's a pretty intimate gesture for someone I just met, but I don't mind. It makes me feel warm and gooey inside. "It's good to put a face to all those messages, Crystal." I start to mumble something about my private life staying private, and that's why I can't share or put pictures up on *Kinks*. She puts a hand up to shush me and says, "No worries, baby girl, I understand about anonymity and not wanting your face on *Kinks*, especially such a pretty face. I get it." She reaches over again and grabs my fingers in her hand. "I'm just one of the lucky ones who gets to meet you."

"*I'm* the lucky one." I squeeze the hand that's holding mine.

She lets my hand go and says, "You're very polite. I'm excited to get to know you this weekend."

The server comes back with my coffee, and we order lunch. I order soup and a sandwich, but Mama_Luvs strongly suggests that I order soup and salad instead. "Salad will be more nutritious," she says. I'm not a salad eater, but I change my order. Thank goodness she lets me have blue cheese dressing on it, which is my favorite. And I don't think I'll die from eating a salad, so it's okay.

My nerves settle down as we eat. She never lets the conversation drag, and even in person, I feel like she hears me, that she really listens. We find ourselves laughing when she tells a couple of stories about her cats and their silliness. She makes it sound like they are her children. Maybe they kind of are. And maybe I'm another one.

After lunch, I pay the bill. That's our agreement. She pays for the hotel room, and I pay for all the meals and food. Hopefully, that's an equitable arrangement, and she doesn't end up paying more than me. We leave the restaurant, and I was half hoping she would reach for my hand. She doesn't. Instead, she suggests I get my bag from the car and come up to the room. She hands me a key card to room 5140 on the fifth floor and tells me she'll wait for me there. I run out to my car and get my bag, not surprised at all when the nerves resurface in my tummy as I get off the elevator on the fifth floor. The room is at the far end of a long hallway. I knock on the door to announce my presence and then swipe the key card. The door unlocks, and I step into our shared room.

I am floored by what I see. Mama_Luvs got us a suite, but it looks like an apartment. An apartment that is about the size of the one I rent in Cincinnati. I see a couch and a loveseat, a desk with an executive chair, a kitchen area with a full-size refrigerator, a stove, an oven, and a microwave. I can't see the view from the suite because the heavy curtains in the living room are drawn. If I didn't get too turned around, the view should be of the Mahoning River.

She steps out through a door and says, "Do you like it?"

"This is amazing. I love it."

"Come in and make yourself at home, Crystal."

Stupidly, I realize that I am still standing in the open doorway, bag in hand. I know that when that door closes, this will become very real. I commit and let the door close behind me. I walk to the curtains and pull them aside, and sure enough, the river is right there across the road. "Mama_Luvs, have you seen this?"

"I have. It's quite a view. And, please, Crystal, just call me Mama, okay?"

"Yes, Ma'am." I feel the blush on my face grow. "Yes, Mama."

"Good girl," she says. "The bedroom has the same view. C'mon, it's this way."

She points to the room she just came out of and heads back toward it. I follow her and am floored by the size of it. It is way bigger than my bedroom at home. The king-size bed is the room's focal point, but there is ample space for the two overstuffed chairs, another desk, and two dressers.

"Go ahead and put your things away." She points to one of the dressers. "The bathroom is right there if you want to freshen up. As for me, I'm going to sit and put my feet up. I'm not used to being in the car that long." She heads over to one of the overstuffed chairs and plops in it. "Ahhh," she says, shimmying to get comfortable.

Once again, I think how striking she is with her confident demeanor. She's reading a brochure, which, for some reason, calms me, and that is a good thing. I place my meager things in one of the empty drawers in the dresser and hang up the two dressy shirts I brought in case we end up going out for dinner or something. I head to the bathroom and do, indeed, "freshen up." After relieving my bladder, I wash my face and hands and then brush my teeth. It wouldn't do to have bad breath, now would it? A quick brush through my hair, and I grab my plastic refillable water bottle to show her that I've been a good girl and drinking water like she asked me to.

"Look, Mama." I hold up my half-empty water bottle. "See?"

"Good job," she says. "Come, sit." She pats the footstool in front of her.

I sit facing her, and I like that I am physically lower than she is. She is setting the tone of our D/s relationship.

She looks down at me. "You are a very pretty young lady, Crystal. I'm surprised no one has snatched you up yet. Do you snore or something?"

I laugh and shake my head. "No, Ma'am. Not that I've been told."

She chuckles and says, "Well, I do snore, so be ready for that. It's best if you fall asleep before I do."

"Duly noted." I get brave and say, "So I assume we'll be, um, sleeping together here?" I gesture toward the bed.

"Is that all right?" She peers down at me over her reading glasses.

"Yes, Ma'am. That's all right."

"Good, good. Now, I figure while we're here in beautiful Marquestown, Ohio, we should see some sights. I hear there is a lovely museum nearby, so we'll visit that and maybe do some shopping downtown. Someone in this room doesn't own a vibrator, and we need to rectify that."

"Mama, what do you mean?" I squint my eyes shut. We are *not* going shopping for a vibrator, are we? Oh, my God.

"No one knows you here, Crystal. No worries." She reaches down and cups my chin so that I am forced to look up at her. "But first things first." I am not sure what she means, and I know my eyes betray me. "Unlike Mistress Ciara, I let you get comfortable and explore your surroundings for a while. But it's time."

"For?"

The smile drains from her face, and she fixes me with a severe Mom stare. Her head cocks to the side slightly, and her eyebrows rise as if telling me I should know. As I look up at her, I can tell that although she uses a stern voice, she has genuine affection for me and won't hurt me knowingly. She is as much excited by our relationship as I am.

"Do you want me to disrobe, Ma'am?" Despite knowing she will take care of me, I hear the shakiness in my voice.

She nods once. "And I won't remind you again." She lets go of my chin.

"Yes, Ma'am." And so, it begins. "But, Ma'am?"

"Yes, baby girl?"

"If I'm not sure of something, you know, like maybe something you think I should know, will it be all right if I ask for confirmation?"

"Yes, of course. That would be a wonderful and grownup thing to do, young lady." I see something like pride in her eyes, and that, more than anything, warms me all over.

From the footstool where I am sitting, I unbutton my shirt and take it off. I leave my bra on and then stand up to take off my shoes and socks and then remove my black jeans. I stand before her in my boi shorts and bra, and she gestures for me to keep going. I remember to breathe and, with a practiced hand, pull my sports bra off, revealing my breasts. My nipples harden in the cool air, and she smiles. I toss the bra on the growing pile and hook both thumbs into the band of the boi shorts. I slowly push them down to my knees and then let them fall the rest of the way to the carpeted floor. I kick them onto the pile.

"Fold all of those neatly and put them away," she says with a commanding but gentle Mom's voice.

"Yes, Ma'am." I fold the clothes, put them in the dresser, and then slide my shoes underneath. I walk back and stand in front of her. I'm not sure what to do with my hands as she looks over my body from top to bottom.

"Sit, baby girl." She gestures to the footstool again. I sit. "Massage my feet, please."

"Yes, Ma'am." I adjust the footstool so that I'm at a comfortable distance, and she puts her right foot on my knee. I put my hands on either side of her foot and rub both ankles before working my way up her foot. I make sure to give her heel some proper attention. "Your feet are dry, Mama," I say, but never stop my rubbing.

"Mm hmm. Next time, we'll use some lotion or oil."

I use my thumbs to press lightly into the sole of her foot, and she seems to purr at that. Yay, I'm doing something right. I become more and more sure of myself with each passing moment. Soon enough, she pushes her other foot into my hand, demanding equal attention.

"Calves, please," she says after a few minutes. She doesn't even open her eyes.

"Yes, Ma'am." I feel a surge of arousal because I seem to be pleasing her. I abandon her left foot and travel up the calf on that side. "You have strong calves, Mama."

"Mmm," is all she says.

I reach her knee, and she says, "Other leg, please." I oblige and work my way up her right calf to her knee. "Higher." Arousal settles low in my belly at this command. I like that Mama is more subtle about her needs. More subtle than Mistress Ciara was.

My hands move up her toned thigh, and there is no mistaking where this is all leading. I move to the other thigh without being told. Her skin is tight, her muscles firm, and I am wet with desire. Feeling bold, I say, "May I kiss you here, Mama?"

"Do you want to?"

"Oh, yes, Ma'am."

She reaches down and tousles my hair. "What a good girl you are. Yes, you may kiss me there."

I kiss as far up her inner thigh as her wool skirt allows me. I push up at it, and she takes the hint and rises high enough for me to push the skirt past her princess parts. I am surprised but not surprised that Mama is not wearing panties.

She skooches forward in the chair and separates her legs wider. I resume my trail of kisses up her left inner thigh and then head to her right. Her musky scent is intoxicating. I kiss and lick my way up her thighs like the good little submissive that I am. I finally reach her center and kiss her squarely on the lovely folds before me. I kiss higher, making direct contact with her tight, hard nub, which elicits a moan from her. This spurs me on. I open my mouth and wrap my lips around her mound and suck her clit gently. I use my tongue and run a wet, sloppy lick across the top. I harden my tongue and flick at it

133

several times. Sensing she is not quite ready for that much attention there, I pull back and lick all around her princess parts as if coloring in the object of our mutual desire. Without warning, I plunge my tongue inside.

"Oh, yes, baby girl. Yes, yes, yes." Mama grabs my head lightly and strokes my hair as if petting me. "Such a good girl," she murmurs. My pussy becomes soaked by her praise.

I plunge my tongue over and over again until it is tired. For a break, I suck in Mama's already soaked lips. I slide my tongue lazily over her fleshy skin. I move to the other side and do the same. I have forgotten how tiring giving girl head can be, so I wrap my arms around her thighs and pull her closer. She moans pleasurably at my dominant move, which empowers me even more. I stick out my tongue and find that little bit of soft skin between her vagina and tiny hole and press my tongue against it. I then move my entire head up slowly, making sure to flick her clit at the top. I must be doing something right because Mama bucks her hips to my rhythm. "Fuck," Mama groans. "That's good, little girl."

I do this whole head maneuver several times until her hands tighten on my scalp, and she directs me to her clit and holds me there. I suck the nub, flick it, then circle it with my tongue until my jaw is reaching the point of exhaustion. Her legs tense up around my head. Her hips buck against my face, so I keep my tongue stiff for her to use. She rubs her clit against my face and tongue and says, "Suck, baby. Suck." I plunge in and suck for all I am worth.

Her orgasm seems to come from her toes as she crushes my head between her thighs. I am held fast as her body jumps and shakes. She moans, but my ears are buried, so I am denied the full sound of her cumming.

She loosens her grip on my head, and I sit back. Her eyes are closed when she sighs a very contented sigh. "That was special, baby girl. Thank you." She opens her eyes and smiles at me, and I puff up with pride. "Go wash up. On your knees when you come back."

"Yes, Ma'am." I stand up and head to the master bath. Before washing, I look at myself in the mirror. My mouth, nose, chin, and cheeks are wet with her essence. I smile at this. I am a happy little slave.

After cleaning up, I head back out and kneel before her. Her legs are still wide open, which I find kind of funny. She is snoring lightly, so I put my hands on my thighs and slump down to be moderately comfortable. I take this moment to study her. Even as she dozes, she has a commanding air about her. I wonder if she was ever in the military. That's the kind of vibe she gives me. Or maybe Moms are just generals whose armies are their children and families. She has a confidence about her that makes me want to stay close. Her eyes are closed, but I know they are brown and full of life. Her brown hair is thick and healthy, with soft waves reaching her collarbone. It shines with vitality, just like the rest of her. Her hawklike nose is strong, too. I'm not sure how a nose can be strong, but it suits her and is just right. I notice that she wears no lipstick or anything else on her lips. Still, her lips don't need enhancing. They have a natural attractiveness. As I close my eyes, I wonder if I will get a chance to kiss those lips this weekend. I relax into mindful breathing. Something tells me I am going to need this rest.

Chapter 14
All Baby Girls

"What a pretty sight," Mama says.

I open my eyes and smile up at her from my kneeling position. She closes her legs and pushes her skirt back down. "Do you know what all baby girls have in common, Crystal?"

"No, Mama." It sounds like the beginning of a joke. "What?"

"They all like to spread their legs wide open. They like to put their princess parts on display."

That wasn't what I expected her to say. "They do?"

"Stand up, legs apart."

I do so and know I am about to be inspected.

"Hands behind your head," she says in a tone that conveys I should have known to do this. "Now."

I follow her instructions, and the posture lifts my breasts nicely, which is good because I'm being analyzed.

"Spread those legs wider," she says sternly. "You know you want to."

I shuffle my feet apart. She reaches out and lays the palm of her hand flat on my not-very-toned belly. "We'll work on this." She gives my flab a shake, and my mood deflates. I think I've severely disappointed her, but I try not to let it show.

She pats my belly once more and then runs a hand up my torso to one of my breasts. She slides underneath and lifts as if weighing it. I am a C-cup size, so she has a nice handful there. "Very nice breasts, baby girl."

She leans closer, and I thought she was going to kiss my breasts, but to my great disappointment, she only runs a finger across the already hardened nipple. I can't help my moan. My nipples have always been sensitive. She cups the breast with both hands and clamps down in one swift move, squishing it between them. I cry out more from the suddenness of it.

"Pain, too. Baby girls like pain, don't they?"

I'm breathing through the pain, so it takes me a moment to answer. "Yes, Ma'am. They do."

She runs a rough thumb over my nipple, and the mixture of pleasure and pain has me squirming where I stand. If I wasn't wet already, I am now.

She drops my breast, reaches into the pocket of her skirt, and pulls out a chain. The chain has clamps on it. She holds both clamps to my lips. "Kiss the object of your desire, baby girl."

I kiss the cold metal, and she wastes no time. The first clamp bites into my hardened nipple, making me jump. The second clamp bites just as hard. As I breathe through the pain, she lets the chain drop. I inhale through my teeth and moan as my body translates the pain into pleasure. The clips are holding fast, and it is then that I realize there are two more clips attached to the other end, making it kind of heavy. I guess anything hanging from someone's nipples would feel heavy.

"Take off your earrings," she commands. I try to move slowly so the weighted clamps don't sway. I am semi-successful. I place both studs in her outstretched hand and put my hands back behind my head before she can tell me to. She puts my earrings next to my phone on the dresser for safekeeping. She reaches down and picks up the other two clamps, relieving the weight. "These will bring you pleasure if you let them, Crystal. Kiss them. That's it. Good girl. Now let your head fall forward," she says. "You're my big, strong girl. You can take it." She attaches one of the clips to my right earlobe, and I gasp at the pain. "Breathe through it. It's on the meaty part. You're all right." After a few moments, the pulsing pain lessens, and my breathing isn't as labored until she snaps the other one on my left earlobe.

"Fuck," I blurt.

"Bad girl." Mama reaches around and swats my ass once. "I abhor cursing. That's one demerit. I will be keeping count."

"Sorry, Mama," I say while trying to catch my breath.

"Oh, yes, you *will* be sorry. Punishments always happen first thing in the morning. This way, baby girls have to think about what they've done all night long."

"Yes, Ma'am."

"Hands down now."

Oh, good. I was getting tired. One thing I realize for sure is that I am *not* in shape. Being a submissive is hard work. No one mentioned any of this in the manual.

"Sit on the edge of the bed far enough back so you can put your feet up and keep your legs spread open.

"Yes, Ma'am." I'm not exactly sure what she wants until she tells me to lay back and lift my pelvis. I gasp when my head falls back, and the chain connected to my earlobes jerks my nipples hard. I moan through the agony for a few moments, but once the throbbing pain in both my nipples and my ears subsides somewhat, I realize that the enticing pulses in my pussy continue.

Mama thrusts a pillow under my ass, and now my princess parts are on display for her to inspect.

"Wider," she says matter-of-factly, and I spread my legs farther apart. I feel my entire body blush. To be on display like this is, I don't know, one part exhilarating and one part terrifying.

Mama runs her hands up my thighs. "We'll work on strengthening these, too." She moves to my inner thighs and teases me mercilessly by coming close to where I want her hands but never quite touching. Her head moves closer, and I know that she must have caught my aroused scent by now. Even I can smell my desire. She puts on her reading glasses, and I'm burning with shame. I'm an object to be inspected. Just like One in that book we're reading together.

"Very nice, baby girl. Beautifully swollen and glistening lips. Baby girl is wet. Her legs are spread wide open, sharing her most private parts. She wants someone to make use of that glistening hole between her legs. Baby girls don't even care what gets put in their holes, just as long as something does. Isn't that right, little one?"

My breathing is getting heavy with her words. "Yes, Mama. It's true." She is basically calling me a slut without saying the actual word.

"Reach down and open those lovely lips. Spread yourself for me."

A surge of excited embarrassment flows through me as I reach down. My thumb and middle finger slide through my wetness, and I pull my lips up and out to the sides displaying my open pussy. I feel dirty but aroused at the same time.

"Ah, good girl. Nice and slick." She looks up at me and adds, "Like a pink and gooey candy center." She leans back and takes her glasses off. "Turn over," she says. "On your knees. Pussy toward me."

I try to answer, but the words get caught. I clear my throat. "Yes, Ma'am." She watches me as I sit up gingerly, trying not to tug at the nipple clamps. I maneuver carefully and am on my hands and knees as she asked. Gravity pulls my breasts down. The chain between earlobes and nipples is taut and is agonizing. I breathe through this exquisite torture. I know I can use my safeword at any time. We discussed this in low tones at the restaurant and decided that the stoplight system was easiest for both of us. I think I'm okay. For now.

"Move farther up on the bed," she says. "Yes, that's far enough. Good girl."

I can't see what she's doing, but I hear her moving behind me, opening zippers, and pulling things out of bags.

"You are a beautiful piece of art, baby girl," she says. "Waiting there so patiently. Wondering what Mama has in store for you." She chuckles, obviously enjoying the power she holds over me. I'm pretty sure she enjoys my discomfort most of all.

"Mama," I say, "these, um, clamps are kind of tight."

"They are, aren't they?" And that's all she says on the matter. She knows that if it is unbearable, I will call out red or yellow to pause things for a moment. "Now, my lovely, our room in this hotel is remote, but sound does travel." She comes up to the head of the bed so I can see her. "You told me you've never worn a ball gag before, and so this is your lucky day." I groan. "Awww, you'll be fine. See these holes in the ball? They will help you breathe. Oh, and remember to snap your fingers if you need to safeword out, okay?"

"Yes, Ma'am," I say, hearing the unenthused tone in my voice. I know she hears it, too, but doesn't comment.

She nestles the ball inside my mouth, and I can't believe how freaking huge this thing is. My tongue is jammed up against it, and I can kind of swallow, but not well. Great. Now I'm going to drool. She straps the gag on firmly by adjusting a strap around my head. Her actions cause the nipple clamps to lift, but I barely notice because I'm trying to adjust to this silicone thing lodged in my mouth.

"Oh, that must be uncomfortable," she says. "Here, let's get you some relief." She unclamps the chains from my ears, and the blood rushes back into them. It's the weirdest feeling, and I ride the pain. Then she takes the clamps off my nipples, and once more, I groan with the pain, my core bracing as if my body is under attack. I fall to my elbows on the bed, trying to breathe through and around the gag. My groans are muffled. I get it now. Ball gags are very effective, but they kind of suck.

"Up on your hands, dear." I rise, fearful for what's next. "Your breasts are lovely swaying to and fro like that." She pushes gently on my arm to make my breasts rock back and forth. Then she takes me entirely by surprise and snaps a clamp back onto the nearest nipple.

Not fair, I protest silently. It burns this time and is not fun.

She moves to the other side and reattaches a clamp to the other nipple. I suck in hard against the gag. The drool is already building up, which is also not fun. I lower my head, thinking that she wants to reattach the clamps to my earlobes, but she doesn't.

"Down on your elbows again," she says. "And this is where you'll probably want to stay for all the things that come next." Oh, no. There's that chuckle again. "Spread those legs, baby girl. You know you want to present your pussy to me. Ahh, that's it. Good girls get rewarded."

She reaches into my wetness and, with two fingers, grabs onto my pussy lips. She tugs slightly, and then, just as I realize what's happening, she attaches one of the clamps to the inner and outer lips on one side. My breath comes hard and fast through my nose as I manage the torture. My ass is sticking straight up in the air, and she rubs both cheeks almost lovingly. It's comforting, but she is both torturing and soothing me at the same time. It is an odd juxtaposition.

As expected, the second clamp goes on the lips on the other side, and I am flayed open. My vaginal hole feels the cool air of the hotel room. It's odd being exposed this way.

"Do you know what comes next, baby girl?"

I hesitate before moving my head, but remember the clamps are no longer attached to my ears. I shake my head.

"All baby girls want to be fucked. That's all they ever want. If they could lean over a grocery cart in the produce aisle with their pussy exposed, inviting the next person that comes along to shove something in their holes, they would. Oh, you know it's true." She rubs my ass with both hands as she taunts me.

The mattress moves as she climbs on the bed behind me. Oh, God, let her have a strap-on. One hand grips my hip. My breathing is shallow and labored. I feel the tip of something at my entrance. There will be no resistance since my pussy lips are tacked open. She pushes in an inch, and then both hands grab my hips. She doesn't move for a moment and then pushes in another inch and stops again. It is agonizing, but I love it. When I use dildoes on myself, I always know what I'm going to do. With Mama, I haven't a clue.

"So unsatisfying," she says. "Only an inch or two. I truly feel bad for guys with small dicks. They can never truly satisfy a woman, can they?"

I have no idea. Hopefully, they're good at licking pussy. But I can't tell her any of my thoughts because I have a big ball in my mouth. And, actually, I don't care because she starts pushing until she's all the way in.

I groan when she bounces up against my cervix. My breasts try to bounce but are halted by the chain attached to my nether lips. Oh, this is agonizing. She pulls out, and I feel the motion of her body behind me. She pushes back in slowly as if gauging my receptiveness. I moan when she bottoms out again. I can feel her naked thighs against my own. The pace of her thrusts increases. My breasts are tortured with every movement, and I moan in perfect rhythm with each push. Her hands leave my hips, and she grabs the flesh of my ass. She grips the flesh so hard that I know there will be bruises. I almost feel like she's channeling her anger into her grip or something. She uses my ass cheeks as leverage to push and pull me back and forth on her phallus. She lets go with one hand and smacks my ass. I jump at the surprise of it.

"Oh, yes," she purrs. This is turning her on immensely. "So good." She slaps me again with every thrust. Finally, after forever, she switches hands and slaps the other ass cheek as hard as the first. Her rhythm doesn't let up as she reaches around my torso and unclips first one nipple clamp, then the other. Relief floods through me, and I fall on my elbows. "Up, girl, up." I rise back up on my hands. She leans forward and drapes herself over my body, grabbing my breasts for leverage. She continues thrusting, although the thrusts don't feel as deep anymore. She is heavy on top of me, and I don't know how long I can bear her weight.

It is then that I feel the flash of orgasm deep inside. I moan as the sensations build. And then Mama does the most unthinkable thing one can imagine. She pulls out, leaving me panting on the bed. "Mama," I cry in frustration, but the gag muffles the word.

"Aww, poor little thing. Didn't get what you wanted?" She grabs my wet inner thigh and squeezes tight. "Baby girls with demerits don't get to cum. I thought you'd figured that out."

I groan. What is it with Dommes and denying orgasms? I wish that weren't a thing. "Mama," I cry again, knowing the word is unintelligible behind the gag. My pleas will do no good, anyway. I start bucking my hips, wanting her back inside me. All that earns me is a sharp slap on my already sore ass and an evil laugh. Mercifully, she undoes the ball gag and takes it out. To my embarrassment, I can't help a long string of drool that leaks out. I wipe my mouth and swallow several times, trying to forget the gag experience.

I feel something cold on one of my ass cheeks. Oh, my God, she's writing on me. "I'm keeping a tally of how many objects I ravage this hungry pussy with. I wrote 'Pussy' and drew a dark arrow to your gaping hole in permanent marker. And then I made one tally mark. I'm sure I'll add to it during our visit over the next two days. Don't you think?"

"Yes, Ma'am," I say.

"Oh, hey, while I'm here," she says as if in deep focus, "I might as well do the same for your asshole." She moves the marker to my other ass cheek, and I feel her writing on my skin, and then I feel the long arrow she draws across my cheek and down to my tiny hole. I have no idea what she's doing next, but I hear the cap go back on the marker. Then she tucks it inside my vagina. "Oops, I guess that'll have to be two tally marks now, won't it." She chuckles deeply and says, "Hmm, while I'm here …" Oh, no. These words are becoming a theme with her. The marker, wet from my vagina, presses against my tiny hole. When it doesn't go in, she swirls it around the entrance. "Loosen up. All baby girls like both holes penetrated. We both know that." She pushes against my hole again and, this time, gains entry. I'll have to be sure to make a tally mark for this. Oh, and by the way, it's going in cap out in case you're worried. I never hurt my little ones."

I hope she means that. She rustles around in a plastic box of some kind, but I can't see what she is doing.

"That was a black permanent marker," Mama says. Let's see if we can get the whole rainbow in your ass. Tell me, smart one, what are the rainbow colors?"

Oh, my God. What is she about to do? I try not to groan as I say, "Red, orange, yellow, green, blue, violet."

"Ahh, taking a shortcut? There are seven colors. You forgot indigo. Aww, that's two demerits now. Lying to your Mama, taking shortcuts. This is unacceptable, Crystal. You'll be punished tomorrow morning for these demerits. But for now, I have a rainbow to see to."

One by one, a marker dips into my wetness and is then inserted next to the original black marker. Every so often, she moves one or more of the markers, causing me to writhe, but it feels good. I buck my hips slightly as she does this. She slaps my ass and tells me to stop. "Oh, and by the way, each one of these has been sanitized. So, no worries there. Mama knows how to take care of her baby girls."

Well, that's good to know. I just hope it's true. I feel my tiny hole stretch impossibly wider as she inserts another marker, but since there is little pain, I don't safeword out.

"Ahh, I think you're at full capacity, little one. The only ones I can't get in are the indigo and violet." She rubs my ass cheeks and sighs in a way that tells me this rainbow exercise of hers has turned her on. "Two more demerits for not fitting the last two markers. Oh, I wish you could see how colorful this is. Your clamped-open pink slit. Your ass filled with most of the colors of the rainbow. It's beautiful. Too bad we agreed not to take photographs. A picture of this could win a contest, I think." She laughs, but it is kind of her own private joke since I can't see her award-winning creation.

She uncaps another marker and then adds more tally marks to my ass cheeks. "I would love to make you wear these colors when we go out, but that would make sitting impossible, wouldn't it?"

"Yes, Ma'am," I say. I'm afraid to say anything else in case she's in a demerit-giving mood.

"But now that you're stretched, let's not waste it." She rummages around in her bags and then pulls the markers out of me one at a time. The unmistakable coolness of lube is applied in and around my stretched hole.

And then something is pressed against it. A butt plug, it has to be, unless she's inserting a rolling pin from the kitchenette or something. "This you *will* wear out to the museum and shopping and dinner." After a few twists and constant pressure, the plug is lodged inside me. She makes another tally mark and then says simply, "On your back."

I flop down on my stomach and then roll over. She is still wearing her top, but her skirt is gone, and so is the strap-on. She reaches over for the clips attached to my lower lips, and I think she will end my agony, but no. How could I believe that? It's too logical. Instead, she adjusts the chain and attaches the dangling clips to my inner thighs. I arch my back and groan at the new pain. My pussy pulses. I do a few Kegel exercises, hoping I can tip myself over into orgasm, but I can't. God, I wish I knew how to have one of those hands-free orgasms.

Mama climbs back up on the bed and makes her way slowly toward my head. "Mama is horny again. Take care of me."

She positions her pussy right over my mouth, and I lift my head to taste her for the second time that afternoon.

Chapter 15
Break

"Satisfied?" Mama asks me.

I tap my full belly and say, "Yes, Ma'am. The food here was good." Okay, that is a bald-faced lie. I hated every single thing, but I'm hoping there will be dessert in my near future. Apparently, volcano fudge brownies are the signature dessert at this downtown restaurant, where I currently sit sipping water. She hasn't suggested dessert yet, and I am not going to ask. I have four demerits already, and I am not interested in more.

"I'm glad you're full," she says. "But remember. You don't ever want to overeat. The stomach is only so big, and when you put in too much volume, it has a hard time handling all of that. Not to mention what it does to your intestines."

Except for the butt plug that I'm ready to rip out, my body feels good. Well, my tastebuds do feel compromised, having to do with the fact that Mama ordered *for* me. I thought it was cool at first. It made me feel special. She was taking care of me. But she never asked me what I wanted or asked me what I liked. She ordered salmon with asparagus tips and a walnut kale salad. Fish? Really? C'mon. No one likes fish, especially not me. And honestly, if I had been the cave person in charge of tasting things, I would have put kale on the poisonous list. It is that bad. But I ate almost all of it and everything else. I didn't want demerits, and I didn't want to offend Mama. But, yikes, that's one meal I've been cheated out of in this lifetime. Mama said that unless you have an allergy to something, it is fair game to eat, so I ate it all, trying not to make faces or gag. But seriously, that kale was not fun.

The only other things that are not happy on my body are my feet. Mama parked in front of the adult toy store, and I thought we were going there first. Much to my consternation, we walked from there to the museum, which had to be over two miles away. After the museum, we walked all the way back. I was seriously ready to order an Uber and even suggested it. She didn't respond, and once we were back at the car, she beamed at me and said, "See? Now when we're done at the shop, the car is right here." Clever. But my feet are now raw and might even be blistered. The shoes I brought to wear with my dressy clothes are not made for urban hiking. Next time, I'll know better.

Thank goodness she drove us to the restaurant because I don't think my feet or legs could have taken any more. The server leaves the bill on the table, and I reach for it. Mama doesn't stop me, of course, because of our agreement. I have been trying not to let her see my credit card throughout our afternoon because my real name is stamped on it. She hasn't asked me, nor have I asked her what her real name is. I am sure this is a bad, bad, bad idea when meeting a stranger for sex. But I have been faithfully checking in with Lisa and Miss Olga so they know I am safe. Mama knows all about it, and she's okay with it.

I put my credit card on the tray upside down and position it away from Mama behind my water glass so she doesn't have a clear view of it. And it's not that she has been trying to see it or anything. I'm just a tad bit paranoid.

Mama takes a sip from the coffee she ordered. I wasn't allowed coffee this evening because she's afraid it would interrupt my sleep cycle. When I asked if I could have morning coffee, she said that was okay.

"Crystal, what was your favorite part about the Art Institute?"

"Oh, so many things," I say. "I don't usually take the time to go to museums, you know?"

"That's something you need to work on, baby girl."

"Yes, Ma'am, I know. But to answer your question, I liked the Norman Rockwell painting of Lincoln."

"The Railsplitter."

"Yes. I had no idea Rockwell was born in 1894." I was surprised to read that on the placard next to the painting. "But, Mama, I have to tell you that my absolute favorite was the Mary Cassatt painting of the mother and her baby. I mean, it wasn't a posed portrait, you know? She captured a genuine moment between a mother and her child. It was perfect." I splayed my hand over my heart. "It really touched me." Mama's warm smile makes me tear up just a little. The painting made me think of how much I miss my real mom.

Mama pats my forearm in comfort and says, "Did you know that Cassatt was instrumental in bringing Impressionism to America?"

I clear the tears from my throat. "No."

Mama nods and adds, "I'm glad I was able to bring her paintings into your world, Crystal."

"Thanks, Mama. I appreciate that." I jump when the server picks up my credit card from the table. She must have overheard me address Mama as Mama. Oh, wow. I wonder what she's thinking. Well, it doesn't matter. I'll never see her again. I don't live in Marquestown.

In no time, Mama and I are back in her car, heading for a grocery store near the hotel. I'm surprised it's still open on New Year's Eve, but it is. This will be our last stop. She wants to buy breakfast items so we don't have to run out first thing in the morning.

"Let's make short work of this," Mama says when she pulls up at an organic grocery store. "We have a vibrator purchase to try out when we get home." Before she opens the door to get out, she turns her head to look at me and says, "How's your plug holding up?"

It was not what I was expecting her to say, and I almost laugh. "I, uh, it's fine."

"Not hurting? Not chafing? Not feeling like you want to push it out?"

"Well, to be honest, I would like it out of me, yes. It's been hours." I hate the fact that she's now made me super aware of it.

"We're almost home. You can hang in there a few more minutes."

"Yes, Ma'am. I can." I follow her into the store, and she puts me in charge of pushing the little half-cart. She is a whirling dervish as she puts items that are foreign to me in the cart. I thought I knew what fruit looked like, but apparently, I don't because whatever she put in the cart does not look like anything I've ever seen before. She puts organic coffee in the cart but ignores me when I suggest half-n-half. Something tells me tomorrow morning's coffee and breakfast will suck as much as the dinner did.

I pay for the groceries, and we head back to the car and the hotel. There are only three bags of groceries to bring up, plus the bag with the vibrator in it, and we manage one trip between the two of us. Of course, Mama makes no effort to hide the bag with the vibrator. I think she does this to make me uncomfortable. I mean, she's not exactly flaunting it, but I would have stuffed that bag under my coat or something.

We get in the room, and she says, "Put those groceries away, please. I'm going to freshen up and then sit for a bit."

"Yes, Mama," I say cheerfully and set about my task. I'm not sure if some things should be refrigerated or not, like this box of rice milk. I err on the side of caution and put it in the refrigerator. I put the weird-looking fruit in there, too. The organic free-range eggs look like they'll make a promising breakfast, but the veggie links that look like sausage? Yeah, not so much. I'll worry about that tomorrow, I guess. I fold up the paper bags neatly and tuck them in a cupboard.

"On your knees," Mama barks from the bedroom doorway. She sounds furious.

"Yes, Ma'am." I grab the countertop for something to hang onto as I lower myself onto the hard linoleum floor in the kitchen. My knees protest this new arrangement.

"What did you forget?" Mama moves closer. Her arms are folded across her chest, and she has that head tilt and raised eyebrow thing going on again. I've messed up. I just don't know how. "That's another demerit bringing you up to five."

"What did I do?"

"It's not what you did. It's what you didn't do. Unless we're in public, you are to …"

My eyes fly wide open when I realize. "I'm supposed to be unclothed. Nude before you."

"And why aren't you?"

"I'm sorry, Mama," I stammer as I undo the buttons on my dress shirt. "I was putting away the groceries."

"Putting away groceries can't be done in the nude? Is there something about clothing that makes that job easier?"

I hang my head. "No, Ma'am." I hear the dejected tone in my voice. I have disappointed her again. "I didn't think, Mama. I'm sorry."

"Sorry doesn't cut it, little girl." Her tone is stern and wipes out all the good feelings from the day we shared. "Get those clothes off, folded, put away, and then stand in that corner."

"Yes, Ma'am." I stand up and head toward the bedroom. My shirt and bra are off before I am even at the doorway. I hurry to fold my clothes neatly and put them away. I don't want demerits for untidy clothes. I scurry back out to the living room and stand in the corner of shame.

"Face the wall," she orders. "Palms flat against the wall. No, at waist height. Good. Now, back your feet up until your holes are presented for penetration." My breasts point down toward the hotel room carpet.

Mama rustles around in one of her many bags and walks over to me. She has a chain in her hand. Oh, no, more clips. She reaches under me and rubs my nipples until they're hard. Both clips snap on quickly, and I gasp both times. She tells me to look in her hand. Crap. There are fishing weights attached to the ends of the chain. She tilts her hand, and they fall. I shriek with pain as the weights bounce below me. It isn't long before she places a gag in my mouth. This one is different. It is a bit gag, she tells me. So I can bite down on it, she says.

Why would I need to bite down –

Thwack! I jump at the impact on my ass. The weights hanging from my nipples sway back and forth. I try to speak, to ask her what the hell, but I can't. The gag prevents me. I look back and see she has a paddle.

"Quiet, little one. We're in the living room. The front door is right there."

I nod my understanding, and she rewards me with another thwack. "Ten smacks for being an impudent little girl. Demerits for minor transgressions are one thing, but out and out defiance, I will," thwack, "not," thwack, "have," thwack. The next five paddles follow in quick succession. I haven't got time to register my burning ass when she shoves a dildo deep into my vagina. This dildo is fat and has a base on it. She fumbles around, and then I understand what she's doing when clips are attached to my labia, effectively holding the dildo in place.

Oh, but she's not finished. She rubs lube around the butt plug. Gingerly, she spins and pulls until it comes out. I sigh in relief. That is until more lube is applied, and something else is shoved in my ass. I can't see what it is, but it's thick, and I feel like something is sticking out. It's heavy and pulls on the inserted portion. It's not a bad feeling. I just wish I knew what it was.

"I was going to surprise you later with this, little girl, but Mama couldn't wait." She backs up and surveys her handiwork. "Oh, you look so cute. Let me show you." She rummages through her bags and pulls out a hand mirror. It takes her a moment, but she finally positions it so I can see that I have a

149

foxtail protruding from my ass. "I even have a set of ears for you." She plunks a band on my head, which I'm assuming has fox ears attached to them.

She steps back and chuckles gleefully at her handiwork. I am not sure I like this turn of events because I am *not* into pet play. But I guess maybe she is, and since *she* is the dominant, I will have to ride this wave. "All your holes are plugged up, aren't they, little one?"

I nod. Once.

"Your mouth. Your ass. Your pussy. This will teach you to remember Mama's rules, won't it?"

I nod again, this time twice.

"Good girl."

Somehow, that phrase is losing its power over me. It's probably because I'm tired and haven't had a moment to relax. I had some time to breathe at the museum, though, which was nice.

"Another fifteen minutes, little girl. And then you will have *hopefully* learned your lesson." Her tone suggests that I thwart her authority at every turn, and she is at her wit's end. "I'm going to pull a couple of chairs toward the big picture window. Maybe we can catch some fireworks this evening. Would you like that?"

I nod my head once only. The weights swing and pull at my nipples. I'm so tired that it's not even translating into an enjoyable experience at this point. And I'm sure she knows that.

I try to breathe calmly and not to think about the ridiculous pose she has me in. She has stuffed me. A gag in my mouth, a foxtail in my ass, a rather large dildo filling my vagina, and weights hanging off my breasts. Oh, I am tired. So tired. Without warning, a sob escapes from deep inside my chest. It surprises me, and I hiccup behind the gag. Another sob hits, and tears flow down my face. And I can't even wipe at them. That makes me cry even more. What am I doing here?

"Oh, now," Mama says as she rushes over. "Shh, shh, shh." She takes the gag off and then unclips the weights. "C'mere, c'mere, c'mere." She pulls me up and away from the wall and wraps her arms around me. "Poor baby. I've worn you down. I didn't think you'd break until at least tomorrow morning."

I don't know what she means about wearing me down, but it's true. I guess she did. I sob in her arms for a few more moments, not knowing where it's all coming from. I finally get myself under control, and she kisses my cheek. "Let's get these things off you." She takes my fox ears off first and then unclips my sore pussy lips, and the dildo falls out on its own. The foxtail plug comes out next. "I'll take care of these things. I want you to shower and put on the pajamas I told you to pack."

I wipe my eyes and then run my hand over my whole face. "Thank you, Mama."

"Go on. Meet me back here in the living room for dessert."

"Really?" My eyes shoot wide open at the mention of dessert.

She nods, and her smile shows genuine affection.

"Okay, Mama. I'll be right back." I zip to the bathroom and wash everything. Some of my bits are more tender than others, but I feel refreshed and rejuvenated when I step out. I pull out the pair of sweats I brought and put on socks. It's been a bit chilly running around nude. I mean, Mama has the heat turned up and all, but I feel cozy with clothes on.

When I head back out to the living room, I see that she has doused all the lights. There are several battery-operated candles here and there, creating a romantic atmosphere. She's pulled two of the living room chairs up to the big window and opened the heavy curtains. The streetlights below are bright, but they don't ruin the mood too much since we're five stories up.

"Come, little one." She pats the chair next to hers and holds up my now-full bottle of water. "Drink some water first, and then –" she holds up a bowl, which I hope contains a good dessert and not kale surprise with sprinkles.

I practically skip over to the chair and plop down in it. She hands me the water bottle, and I drink for a long time. After a bit, she nods, and I take that to mean she is satisfied with my water intake for now. She hands over the dessert bowl, and, holy moly, it looks like vanilla ice cream. "Thank you, Mama. I didn't see you buy this."

"I have my ways, little one."

She reaches over and tousles my hair, and all is forgiven. I take a spoonful of ice cream, and after putting it in my mouth, I realize something is not right with this ice cream.

"Don't you just love sugar-free ice milk? No pesky sugar and fewer calories." She reaches over and pats my belly. I am mortified when it bounces a few times. "See?" she says. "We can have treats, but we must make them

151

good treats."

"Oh, Mama, look. Fireworks." I point out the window. There genuinely are fireworks there, but I need to get the focus off of me. She probably knows what I'm doing, being the Mama, after all, but I don't care.

We eat in silence for a while and watch the colors light up the night sky. She breaks the silence. "Tell me about your mom."

Her words reach through my chest and grab my heart. Tears spring to my eyes, and I swallow back a sob. "Um, she passed from pancreatic cancer." I look down. I can't make eye contact with her. I scrape the spoon along the bottom of the empty bowl.

"When?"

I know she hears me fighting back tears. I swallow hard and say, "A little over five years ago."

"And it feels like yesterday."

"Yes." She understands.

"Grieving is a long process, Crystal. And I don't think we ever stop. Sometimes an event, an object, or even a smell can remind us of the person we've lost, and all those feelings bubble right back up to the surface." She takes the empty bowl from me and sets it on the floor. She takes one of my hands in hers and rubs the back of it with her other hand. My shoulders relax.

"Mama?"

"Yes, sweetie?

"What did you mean when you said I wouldn't break until tomorrow?"

"All baby girls are fragile, little one. You're no exception. You looked for a mama for a reason, I think. And whatever it is that has you locked up and unsure about life had to surface at some point."

"So, you knew I might...?" I look up at her and see a caring expression on her face.

"Well, I didn't know for sure. I mean, you are pretty butch." She waggles her eyebrows to tease me.

I chuckle weakly. "Soft butch."

"You're allowed to have feelings, dear. I'm glad I'm here to comfort you."

"Thank you, Mama."

Her smile is like a warm hug. We sit in silence for a while, watching the fireworks. I can't help but relive the last few months I had with my mom. She was so sick and just not her usual self. It fell to Dad and me to take care of her. He was a little bit in denial, and so I had to take on the brunt of the emotional stuff. He'd hide away in his little cubby of an office and play solitaire on his computer. I worked on my dissertation on my laptop anywhere mom was. Most days, she felt strong enough to watch TV in the living room, but some days, she stayed in bed because the chemo wreaked havoc with her body. I even did schoolwork in the oncology unit of the hospital while she was getting chemo. Tears are starting up again, and I need to get off this line of thinking.

I take a deep breath and let it out slowly. Mama is right. Sometimes, the memories come crashing in unbidden. But now I need to tuck them away and be here and present with the woman sitting beside me.

I take another deep breath and then clear my throat. "Mama?"

"Yes, sweetie?"

"A foxtail?"

She bursts out laughing, and I can't help it; I burst out laughing, too.

Chapter 16
Subspace

Midnight comes, and we wish each other a happy new year. There is no kiss, which disappoints me, but Mama is in charge, and I have to accept it. She makes me disrobe as we get ready for bed. She also undresses, and I steal glances at her breasts. They are lovely and full. Why hasn't she let me touch them yet?

She tells me to kneel on the floor and put lotion on her feet and calves. I think maybe she will want me to dive into her pussy again, but after a while, she takes the lotion from me and does her hands and elbows on her own while I remain kneeling before her.

"Tomorrow morning," she says, "I have to add one more tally mark to each hole for tonight's activities. Hopefully, the permanent marker didn't wash away with your shower."

"It did not, Ma'am," I say. "I was careful."

"Such a good girl," she says. "Okay, go on. Get into bed. I usually make baby girls get up at 5:30 to make the coffee, but I think we'll sleep in tomorrow. How does that sound?"

"That sounds wonderful." I lift up the covers on the other side and crawl in. "Oh, wait. I forgot." I get back up and open the drawer where I stashed him. I pull out my Pooh bear and bring it back with me to the bed.

"Oh, a stuffie," she gushes. "He's a cutie."

I squeeze him tight. Apparently, this means I have permission to sleep with him. Yay.

"You're a lucky little girl tonight."

"How so, Mama?"

"Normally, I chain little girls to the bedpost at night so they don't wander. It's for their safety, of course." Her words floor me, and I don't know what to say. "But you've been through enough this evening."

"Okay. Thank you." My mind desperately tries to make sense of what she just said. Is she teasing me? Or was there a serious note to her statement? I am suddenly wide awake.

"All I ask is that you don't leave the hotel room," Mama says. "I would prefer it if you stay in this bedroom until I wake up in the morning. No wandering around or snooping."

"Okay. Yes, Ma'am." I get the distinct feeling that she is as wary of me as I have been of her. It's not that there is a problem; it's just that being with a stranger has its inherent dangers. And we both seem to know it.

"I've taken melatonin to help me sleep, and I suggest you get on with sleeping yourself."

"Yes, Ma'am." She doesn't respond, so I say, "Goodnight, Mama."

"Goodnight, baby girl."

"Thank you for a nice day."

She pats me on the hip and says, "Go to sleep now."

"Yes, Ma'am."

Although I am exhausted, sleep does not come. It does for Mama, unfortunately, and she was right about her snoring. It is not a soothing sound at all. I don't dare get up to sleep on the couch in the living room because she would be furious with me if she found out.

I doze on and off during the night and take a couple of trips to the bathroom to break up the monotony. I am most certainly not rested when morning comes and she wakes up.

After she goes to the bathroom, she peeks her head out and says, "Assist me in the shower."

She adjusts the water temperature and then steps in. "Get in here." I step in, and she hands me a scrubby and points to the body wash. I wash her body, but she doesn't let me linger anywhere. She washes her hair, rinses, and then turns off the water. She tells me to get on my knees. The tiles hurt. She must know this but doesn't care.

She lifts one leg up and rests her foot on the wall-mounted soap dish. "Do what you do best. Because if there's one thing baby girls must be good at, it is pleasing Mama." I maneuver into position and lick my way up one thigh to her lovely clean pussy. I know it's clean; I washed it myself. I nibble on her lips and dart my tongue inside. She strokes my head as I work. "Baby girls know it's a privilege to suck on Mama's princess parts, to please Mama in a way that only baby girls can." She moans as I hit an arousing spot. "Ahh, yes, only good girls get to lick Mama's pussy. It's their reward for following instructions. For making their holes ready and wet for Mama to penetrate."

My tongue and lips work feverishly on her, and she rocks her hips. We get in a good rhythm, and judging by her soft sighs and moans, her orgasm is building.

"I knew you'd be wet last night. Did you know that? You stood in the corner bent over, presenting your holes to me, and I shoved that dildo inside you. You didn't know it was coming." She moans and grips my head tighter. She wants me to stay on her clit. "Yes, yes, baby girl. Please me. Make me cum all over your face and mark you as mine to do whatever I –"

Her words cut off as she cries out her release and bucks her private parts over my face. I am so pleased with myself for making her cum that I'm almost smiling. She stills her body but laces her fingers in my hair and then moves my head around, coating my forehead, nose, cheeks, and even my hair with her spendings. "Mmm," she moans again. "You are not to wash that off until I tell you to."

"Yes, Ma'am."

She pushes me away and turns on the shower again. "Clean me." She hands me the scrubby. Once I'm finished, I am instructed to remain kneeling on the wet shower floor while she dresses in the bedroom. She comes back in wearing a tight black corset that pushes her breasts up high and on display. Her nipples are hard and enticing. Down below, she wears a short black skirt with dark stockings and high heels. She is stunning. She is fierce. She is a Domme. No. She is *my* Domme, and whatever she wants from me, I will give her.

"We have the matter of five demerits to take care of," she says. She reaches into one of her bags and pulls out an enema box. My heart drops. Again? What is up with Dommes and their enemas? "I will put this solution inside you, and you will hold it for five minutes."

My eyes fly open wide. "Five, Mama?" The last time I did this at Mistress Ciara's, I managed about two minutes tops.

"Five demerits, five minutes." She moves closer and says, "Forehead on the tile, please, ass up, toward me." I move quickly. "Reach back and spread those cheeks wide." The weight of my upper body is now forced onto my forehead, but I do as I'm told. She slides the thin, lubed nozzle into my tiny hole and squeezes. I feel myself filling up. Holy moly, she's going to use the entire bottle inside me. "Stop squirming." She swats my ass in reprimand. "Okay, all done." She pulls the nozzle out. "You can let go of those cheeks." Oh, thank God. I press my hands against the floor tile to help hold my weight.

"Let me start the countdown." She props her phone up on top of the toilet tank so I can see it out of the corner of my eye. She presses start.

The one thing I didn't initially see about her outfit is the crop. At least, I think it's a crop. She rubs the business end across my jawline and then trails it over my shoulder and down my back to my ass cheeks. When it goes away, I know what's about to happen. A quick swat stings my right cheek. I jump.

"Hold your water, young lady," she reprimands.

"Yes, Ma'am," I say and grimace. The first wave of cramping has already started.

Swat. Another sting. This time on the other cheek. She gets into a regular rhythm, and I realize she's using the countdown on her phone to time them. Trying to figure out her timing takes my mind off my very real need to push the solution out. I calculate that she hits me approximately every ten seconds.

I groan as another wave of cramps hits me.

"It will pass," she says calmly and swats my ass again. And true to her word, the cramping does pass. So, if I just ride them out, I'll make it. The urge to go is enormous, but the regular stings from her crop help give me something else to concentrate on. That is until she shoves the crop in my pussy and fucks me with it for almost the entire last minute. "I told you baby girls were always wet," she says smugly.

"Ten seconds," she says and pulls the crop out. "You can move when the alarm sounds. But do not lose a single drop until your ass is over that toilet." She backs away but doesn't leave. Oh, great, she is going to watch me dump the contents of my colon from the doorway. Just great.

When the alarm sounds, I do not leap to my feet. Instead, I get up slowly and carefully. Thank God the lid is already up and the seat down. I hold my breath, and I am on shaky legs but manage to get on the toilet before the torrent exits my body. The cramping continues for a while, and when I'm confident everything is out, I wait a few moments more and then look up at Mama.

She wears a proud smile. "Good job, baby girl. Those demerits from yesterday are now gone. You have paid for them, and we are never going to bring them up again. A clean slate, so to speak."

"Thank you, Mama." It is the weirdest thing I think I've ever said in my lifetime. I'm thanking a woman who made me take a 5-minute enema. Where has my life gone to?

"Clean up those princess parts, brush your teeth, and meet me in the kitchen. You've earned breakfast and coffee."

"Yes, Ma'am," I say enthusiastically. I am starved.

"You are *not* to wash my markings off of your face."

"Yes, Ma'am," I say less enthusiastically.

I clean up but desperately wish I could wash my face. Her cum has dried there and feels weird. I'm not going to look at or touch my hair because I don't want to know. The smell of coffee almost makes me drool as I walk into the kitchenette. She hands me a cup, pours the coffee, and offers me "cream" and "sugar." As I suspected, the "cream" she offers is not half-n-half. It's rice milk. I pour it in and take a sip. I lie when I say, "Mmm, this is good, Mama. Thank you." Rice milk is not a substitute for real coffee creamer. Ever.

"See? Substitutes for favorite foods don't have to be bad."

"I have a lot to learn, I guess." That, at least, is true.

"Now, when we finish our coffees, I'll make us breakfast, and you, baby girl, will do crunches while I'm cooking."

"Crunches, Ma'am? As in sit-ups?"

She nods and sits down at the little table in the kitchenette. She pats the seat next to her. "Oh, yes. You have some baby fat to lose. No sub of mine is going to be slovenly and out of shape."

"Yes, Ma'am," I say, trying my best not to sound dejected. I wish we could just talk or something and not focus on my inadequacies. "Mama?"

"Yes, sweetie?"

"Before I do crunches, will you add last night's tally marks to my body?"

She puts her coffee cup down hard on the table, and I wince. Oh, God, what did I say wrong now? It's a demerit, for sure. "Good girl, Crystal. I told you to remind me, and you did. Mama completely forgot. Go get the bin of markers." She points to a small plastic box on the coffee table. "They're all cleaned and sanitized now, so don't worry."

I retrieve it and place it on the kitchen table.

"Go put it on the bed. I'll adjust your numbers later when we play."

"Yes, Ma'am." I scurry into the bedroom and put the box smack in the middle. I scurry back and sit next to her. I take another sip of coffee.

"Coffee is a wonderful gift," she says. "Some say it's proof that God loves us."

I chuckle. "I think so."

"Have you ever had a coffee enema?" I shake my head. "Ooh, you're in for a treat. We'll do that tomorrow."

Joy.

We both drain our cups at the same time, and she says, "Would you like another cup with breakfast?"

"Oh, yes, please," I say, trying to sound like a good girl. Bad girls who have demerits don't get orgasms. And I desperately want one. I *need* one. I haven't had one since my arrival.

"Off you go. Crunch time." She points to an open space on the living room floor.

I lay down there and start doing the ordered crunches. This reminds me of my college softball days – crunches, pushups, and burpees on the dorm room floor. I haven't done anything like that in a long, long time. And I definitely never did them naked. Mama didn't ask me to count, but I'm doing it silently, anyway, just in case she asks for the final count. I have a nice pace going, but I dare not stop. At one point, when her back is turned away from me, I slow down a little. As soon as she moves, I pick it right back up. She probably knows I'm doing this because moms have eyes in the backs of their heads, but I'm getting tired, and I have to do something to conserve my energy. My core muscles reach the exhaustion point when Mama finally tells me to stop and come to breakfast.

"How many?" she asks.

"Two-hundred and forty-seven." Oh, you don't even know how lucky I feel because I counted.

"That's great. I think that's a baby girl record." She sets two plates down on the table, and I sit down. "You played sports in high school, didn't you?"

"Yes, Ma'am," I say. "Softball in the spring." I don't tell her that I also played in college. The less she knows, the better.

"Excellent. So later, when I make lunch, you'll need to beat 247. And this time, you'll count out loud for me. Cheating baby girls do *not* last long with me." She places my second cup of coffee in front of me, and it looks like she already added the rice milk.

I thank her, put my napkin in my lap, and wait for her to sit.

"Go ahead and eat."

"Thank you, Mama. Everything looks so good." And it actually does. She made eggs over medium, and the sausage links look and taste like real sausage. Maybe this substitute food thing has merit. I don't know. The jury is still out. "What is this fruit, Mama?"

"You've never had papaya before? I have no idea how they got papaya in December, but it's a rare treat."

"I've heard of it. It kind of looks like cantaloupe but tastes very different. It's good." And it is. Except for the rice milk, breakfast is good.

Mama talks about her job a little bit and how difficult it is to work with lazy people. According to her, Millennials are the softest, laziest, entitled beings ever created, and she has no use for them.

I'm a millennial. She knows that, doesn't she? I have to change the subject. "Mama, would you like me to clean up and do the dishes?"

"They're not going to do themselves, now are they?"

"No, Ma'am."

"Go on," she leans back so I can take her now-empty plate away. "I'll be in the bedroom. Join me when you're done."

I make quick work of my chores and take an extra few seconds to make sure everything is perfect, including the dishtowel, which I hang precisely the way I saw her do it earlier. I take another minute to relieve my bladder in the main bathroom, and while I'm there, I rinse out my mouth. I take a couple of deep cleansing breaths to get centered and then take my naked self to the bedroom.

My heart jumps when I see Mama. She is sitting in a chair, looking at me without smiling. Her fingers are steepled and resting against her stomach. Her skirt is gone, and she is sporting a strap-on. The dildo stands straight out, pointing at me. Well, I guess I know what's next.

"On your back." She points to the bed. "Let's see how flexible you are."

I get on the bed and lay on my back.

She picks up a tube of lube and a black marker. "Pull up your knees. Yes, that's it. Now, keep your head back and hug your knees. Roll back so I can update your tallies."

"Yes, Ma'am." I tighten my sore core muscles and pull my ass up, but that's as far as I can go. She frowns and then uses both hands to push me up by my ass cheeks. My feet fly over my head, coming to rest on the headboard.

"Not very strong in your core, are you?" she admonishes. "Baby girls should not be lazy." She climbs on the bed, and I feel her add a few single lines to the tally. She tosses the marker on the side table near the bed.

I stay in my position, ass to the ceiling, hugging my knees.

She squirts lube in and around my tiny hole and on her dildo. "Look at me," she commands. "Let go of your knees and spread your legs." My stomach muscles tighten and complain at all this unfamiliar usage. Once I've done this, she moves her upper body through my open legs and puts one hand down beside my shoulder. With her other hand, she guides the tip of the dildo to my lubed hole. She pushes the dildo against me while watching my face intently. She presses harder but doesn't break through the knot of muscle. Finally, with a persistent push, she breaks in, and my eyes flutter at the momentary pain.

"Good girl," she whispers. "Take it all." She pushes the dildo in slowly. It feels so good going in. She bottoms out and then pulls back. With a steady rhythm, she slides in and out of my clean-as-a-whistle rectum. Every now and then, she pulls all the way out and watches my face as she regains access against the tight ring. I moan at these intrusions but love how it feels. I'm glad Mistress Ciara literally opened me up to this form of pleasure.

Both of Mama's hands are on either side of my shoulders now. Her breasts dance in front of my face. I long to watch them bounce, but Mama said to keep eye contact. She pumps me faster and faster still. My legs open up to let her in deeper. Her body slams into mine.

"Baby girls like to be fucked in the ass, don't they?"

"Yes, Ma'am," I say. My throat is croaky, but I don't clear it.

She slows down her pumping, and with one hand, she reaches up and pulls both of her breasts completely out of the corset. She lowers herself and smashes one of her breasts into my face. "Suckle."

Finally! I have been so hungry to touch her. I use my tongue to pull her nipple into my mouth and suck her hard. I suck to the rhythm she sets as she fucks me. When my sucking muscles tire, I lick her with a soft tongue and then a hardened tongue. Without warning, she swaps breasts. I suck this one in the same way.

And then I feel it. An orgasm is building. I moan, and she whispers, "Touch yourself. I want to hear you cum. Cum like those audio clips you sent Mama."

I reach down and am amazed at how soaked I am. Everything is slippery. My clit is rock hard and fat, and I circle it with fast strokes. Every thrust from Mama electrifies my nerves. Her body hovering over me, possessing me, gives me submissive joy.

Arousal floods me, and my limbs feel like jelly. I am a flying ragdoll heading into an unstoppable vortex. It sucks me in. My mouth opens, and I empty my lungs as the orgasm hits. My body goes rigid. My vaginal muscles spasm tightly as passion floods my hand. I moan with each pulse and am still moaning when Mama pulls out. She moves my legs down so I'm lying flat. My body trembles on the bed as the rest of me flies high around the room.

I become more aware when Mama places her pussy over my mouth. As if in a dream, I suck and lick and penetrate, but I'm not really there. Even when she cums and then smears her wetness all over my face and hair again, I'm still not quite present, preferring to stay floating in space.

"Good fucking whore," Mama murmurs in some far-off distance.

I keep my eyes closed as she now trails her wetness over my breasts and down my torso. I groan when I realize she called me a whore. She's never called me a whore before. I don't know any whores, but I'm sure they're nice people. I smile as my head rolls lazily around the pillow underneath it.

"The whore is in subspace," Mama mumbles, but she's not talking directly to me. Is whore a good thing in her mind or a despicable thing? I don't know. It doesn't matter. I am flying.

I feel her put something on my right wrist, and then she pulls my arm up and over my head. Too late, I realize she has shackled me to the bedpost. She does the same to the left. My arms are spread wide apart. This shoots me out of subspace, and I blink my eyes open.

"Mama?" I yank at the chain. "What's happening?"

She doesn't answer and doesn't even look at me. My heart pounds with adrenaline. She turns her back and heads out the bedroom door, closing it behind her with a soft click.

Chapter 17
Thank Your Mama

When Mama didn't come back for a while, I must have dozed off. I am jolted awake when she pulls my legs apart and attaches a spreader bar between my ankles. She doesn't speak to me while she does this. Without warning, she shoves a big dildo into my vagina and proceeds to fuck me with it by hand. I know I can safeword out, but I don't. My brain rationalizes that she is giving me a slave experience. Oh, God, I hope that's all it is and that she hasn't become some deranged psycho.

I'm a bit nervous and on guard, but I am amazed when my body reacts to the friction she provides. An orgasm builds during her relentless pounding, and I cum, my vaginal walls spasming hard against the silicon phallus. Oddly, it wasn't enjoyable.

She pulls out after I cum and shimmies up my body. I figure she will use my mouth to make her cum, but she doesn't. No, this time, she holds herself up and squats over my chest. She rams a smaller dildo into herself as I watch. She pulls the dildo out and then shoves it in my mouth. She does all of this wordlessly. She fucks my mouth with it a few times, occasionally hitting the back of my throat, and then shoves it back into her vagina. The second time she pulls it out, it drips with her arousal. She physically opens my mouth with her hand, reaches in, and pulls my tongue out with two fingers. She places the dildo on my tongue and rolls it around using my tongue like a napkin. She does this several more times, meaning to degrade me. It's not sexy at all, but it's not something I want to call a safeword over. I am so relieved when she goes back to masturbating and finally cums.

But then she sits on my face. She's heavy. I can't breathe. I thrash around, trying to push her off, but I am unsuccessful. At least I'm able to catch a breath or two. Eventually, she relents and resigns herself to coating me with her cum.

Fine. I don't care because at least I can breathe.

We hadn't built up enough trust for smothering, and as I catch my breath, I try to decide if I should say "Red" or not. She looks at me with an odd expression as if trying to figure out what to do to me next. I watch her every move as she reaches for something on the side table. It's the ball gag. She quietly puts it on me. I guess she is done with my mouth for now. I decide that smothering sucks, but I seem to be okay and keep my safeword to myself. She said she'd never hurt her baby girls, and I choose to believe her. Her silence and non-communication are kind of freaking me out, though. She is something other than a nurturing mommy type right now. I'm just not sure *what* she is.

She leaves the room, and I doze again.

The entire morning and early afternoon are a blur. At one point, she takes off the spreader bar and puts a collar on me. She pulls me to the bathroom so I can relieve my bladder while she watches intently. Then she leads me back to the bed and rechains me face down. She puts ankle cuffs on me and then ties me to the bedposts. I pull on them, and I don't have much leeway. The blows with the crop on my ass and legs are soft and spaced out. The pain feeds my arousal at first, but then, after a while, it burns. I don't use my safeword, or in this case, safe snaps, because I want to prove to her that I am not a soft millennial and that I can take whatever she gives me. I'm grateful she stays away from my kidneys and head and neck areas as we had agreed. This makes me continue to trust her, but honestly, that trust is wearing thin.

After the crop session, she penetrates me with two dildoes, gets bored of that, and shoves those blasted markers in my ass again. If I wasn't so nervous, I might have been proud when she shows me with the hand mirror that my ass has taken all the colors of the rainbow in addition to a black and a brown marker. She paddles my ass next, and it is not good. I start crying, and I just want to go home, but all I do is bury my face in the pillow and pray she will finish soon.

After this debauchery, she pulls the markers out, leaves the room, and shuts the door. Maybe she has to recharge and get her strength back. Impossibly, I doze off, almost fearful about what she has planned for me next.

I wake up with a vibrator against my clit. It's the one I bought yesterday, and it's too much. She puts it right on my sensitive nerve endings, which kind of hurts. My body writhes as I try to move away, but she is skilled and holds that part of me down. She must have a sixth sense because she backs off when I am close to cumming. She finally does make me cum, but it isn't enjoyable. And every time I think it's over, she puts the vibrator back on my clit. I cum over and over again, so many times that I lose count. My nose runs, and drool leaks out the sides of my mouth around the gag. She has exhausted me, and I don't put up any fight. Somewhere in the fog of my mind, I remember what these are called – forced orgasms. They were not on my to-do list. Ever.

What I hope is the end finally comes when she pulls a chair close to the bed. I am on my back again, not remembering how I got that way. She takes the ball gag out of my mouth and throws it somewhere on the bed. I work my sore jaw back and forth to relieve the soreness. It helps, but not much.

She yanks my head in her direction so I can watch her. She opens her legs wide and lazily rubs her labia and clit. I don't make eye contact because I don't want to know what I will see in her eyes. Instead, I wish for my numb princess parts and my crop-burned paddle-beaten ass to recover. I watch her touch herself. It might have been sexy under any other circumstance, and I might have been aroused by it, but I am too much in flight mode to enjoy it.

As I catch my breath, a battle continues to rage inside me. I need to say something to tap out of this nightmare. But what if she ignores me? What if this nightmare is real? So, I don't say anything. Instead, I endure her torture.

"Oh, baby girl," she says, breaking the hours-long silence between us. "You have to put up more of a fight. This almost wasn't fun. Despite that, I see a great future for us. You're such a lovely whore. Just like the baby boys, I nurture. All baby boys are whores, you see. They don't care what you do to them as long as you eventually touch their little pee-pees." She slides her middle finger inside her vagina and rhythmically moves it in and out.

"Mmm," she moans. "I can picture it. You licking my pussy, your ass in the air, and my baby boy putting his hard cock inside you. His hands grip your hips. Oh, how you'll squeal when you finally feel real flesh inside your cunt. Real cum filling you up." She moans again. "My two beautiful babies fucking each other, pleasing Mama."

I pray to God that her "baby boy" isn't making his way up to the room now. I didn't sign up for that. Oh, my God.

"I'll chain his balls to your pussy lips. Every thrust will be beautiful agony for you both." Her hips rock to the cadence of her finger movements. "Mmm, mmm," she moans. Her breathing is labored. I know the signs. She is getting close.

"Oh, baby girl. I have it! You'll suck his cock, deep throat him, all the way down your throat so you can't breathe. His cock will be so far in that he'll drop his load right into your stomach. He shoots a lot of cum, especially first thing in the morning when he's recharged. You'll have to learn how to swallow, baby girl. It'll be hard at first, but you'll get it. It's every woman's lot in life to learn how to swallow copious amounts of cum. It just is."

Her hips buck faster. "You'll deep throat him while I'm behind you, fucking you in the ass. We both know how much you like anal, baby girl. And, oh, oh, oh, won't it be wonderful when my baby boy fucks my baby girl in the ass and cums inside her. He has a massive dick. It's thick, and it's long. He'll fill you up. He might even tear you, but you'll heal eventually.

"Maybe I'll get another baby boy," she muses. "They can both go at you while I watch. One fucking your mouth, the other fucking whichever hole I say. What do you think? Would you like big brothers who have my permission to have their way with you any time they want?"

"Ungh, ungh, ungh," she cries. Her back arches, and she throws her head back. Her bucking pelvis is aimed in my direction as if boasting her sexual prowess and control over me. I look down, not wanting to watch.

She finally uncoils, and it takes a while for her to get her breathing under control.

"I have to pee," I say when I think she's come down.

"Oh, is that so," she says with disinterest. She swipes a hand through her nether regions, leans over, and wipes her wetness across my face, from one cheek across my nose and mouth to the other cheek. I don't flinch when she does this; I stay calm and cool. Neither of which I am. She is trying to degrade me. Some subs get off on this. I'm not one of them. While she was spinning her tale of forced slavery and rape, I made mental notes of where my clothes, shoes, phone, wallet, and car keys are. Everything is basically in two drawers of the dresser or on top of it, ten feet from me.

She dips in her well again and coats my breasts this time, taking a moment to pinch and twist each of my nipples painfully. I don't give her the satisfaction of crying out. She moves to the bottom of the bed, and I think she is about to undo the straps at my ankles, but instead, she grabs my calves and pulls my whole body lower. She lifts one leg on the bed and lowers herself onto my foot. My big toe slides inside her slick folds. A few more toes follow. She grabs my foot, holds it upright, and then literally impales herself on as much of my foot as she can. She moves up and down with small movements and says, "Wiggle your toes."

I do so, and it is the strangest sensation. Warm, slippery, soft, spongy. All of those things. She rubs her clit with her hand and bucks up and down, making my foot fuck her. Her breathing quickens, and then, unbelievably, her walls contract around my foot. "Oh, oh, oh," she moans. "Fucking whore. Fat fucking lazy millennial." The contractions stop, and she lifts herself off my foot.

She reaches down and, instead of merely unclipping the ankle cuffs from the bed, takes both cuffs off me entirely. My ankles are rubbed raw in spots, but I don't care. I lie there with my eyes following her every move as she takes off my collar. She then takes off one wrist cuff and strolls to the other side of the bed. As soon as the other wrist is free, I sit up, pivot, and head calmly to the bathroom. I try to play it cool, even though I am far from it. I know she hears me lock the door. Good. I don't care.

I wash every inch of myself in the shower and pee while I'm in there to save time. I towel off and hope she's not right outside with a chainsaw. I wrap several towels around me in case I have to run out the door without clothes. I take a quick, deep breath to center myself and unlock the bathroom door. I crack it open and don't hear anything. I open it wider and thankfully don't see her in the bedroom.

In a rush, I yank open the dresser drawers and throw on my jeans. I don't bother with panties. My keys, wallet, and phone get stashed in the pockets next. I throw on my sweatshirt and then shove my feet into sneakers, tucking the laces inside without tying them. There's no time. Thinking I hear a noise, I freeze and listen for a moment. No, it's nothing. This can be good, or this can be bad. I shove the rest of my clothes inside my travel bag, making sure I get my Pooh bear. I brush my earrings from the top of the dresser into the bag, too. Oh, God, this is taking too long, but I stop for my two dress shirts in the closet anyway. My winter coat is on a hook by the front door. If I can get that, then I will be batting a thousand.

I walk up to the closed door to the living room and listen. I hear nothing. Maybe she left. I doubt it. She was practically naked when she left the bedroom, and I didn't see her take any clothes with her. Oh, God, I can't believe how fucking naïve I have been. I had no idea how capricious she would be. I shake my head. No, I can't lay blame right now because I am totally not out of danger yet.

I turn the bedroom door handle slowly. I have no idea what I'm going to say, probably nothing, but the plan is to head straight for the front door and grab my coat on the way.

"You're going?" Mama_Luvs says from the living room couch. "We haven't had lunch." She says this calmly, as if she hasn't been abusing me all day. Thankfully, she doesn't get up. I don't want to get physical with her. I stay silent and keep moving toward my target. "You can at least thank your Mama for a good time."

I unlock the front door and open it. I grab my coat and, on a whim, turn around and say, "Red. Crystal out." I head out the door at double speed, not wanting to hear a reply if there is one. She's probably sitting there laughing.

I bolt for the stairs. I will not be stuck in an elevator. I take the stairs two at a time as hiccupping sobs bubble up from inside.

I get out to the parking lot and panic when I can't remember where I parked. My rational mind kicks in, and I remember. My hands shake as I fumble with my keys, but I finally get the car door unlocked. I toss my bag inside, jump in, and slam the door shut. I lock the doors twice. The car starts right up, to my relief, and I squeal the tires as I back out. I pull onto the road and look in the rearview mirror. There is no way she could be following me this fast. I focus on the road and the cars around me. It would do no good to get in a wreck and be stuck here.

Once on the highway, I pull out my phone and see six messages from Lisa and one from Miss Olga. I pull over on the shoulder and text Miss Olga, telling her I lost track of time and that I am all right. I text Lisa the same thing, even though I am far from all right, and ask if I can call her later. She texts back immediately and says she's glad I'm okay and that she'll be waiting for my call.

As I drive home, the smooth cadence of the tires on the road soothes me. I cannot believe how absolutely stupid I have been. Putting faith in a person

I didn't know. And this is the second time I've done it. "Do you have a death wish, Bernadette?" I say this out loud so maybe I'll hear it.

The words reverberate in my mind, and I wonder if they might be true. I once heard the phrase *suicide by cop*. Am I trying to do the same? Suicide by sexual predator? Once I'm more than two hours away from Mama_Luvs, I pull off a busy exit and head to a Hungry Hamlet's fast food joint. I use the facilities, noting how very sore all of me is down there, and then order a to-go meal full of fat and sugar and nothing redeeming.

I look around the parking lot, paranoid that she has somehow been able to teleport here, but all is clear. My heart pounds until I finally get back in the car and lock the doors again. I take a sip of soda and pull out the cheeseburger. After a few bites, I put the burger down and pick up the phone. I can't wait anymore. I punch in Lisa's number.

She answers quickly.

"A wolf in sheep's clothing," I say cryptically.

"Are you all right, B?" Lisa asks.

"Yes. I –" My words get caught in my throat. "Yes, I'm fine. Now."

"Tell me."

I proceed to tell her how Mama_Luvs was charming at first and Mama-ish, which I liked, but things were a little weird right from the start. "I chalked it up to nerves and meeting her for the first time. But then something came over her, and she turned, I don't know, mean or something."

"Did she hurt you?" There is an aggressive growl to her voice, which made me feel good. Protected.

"N-no."

"You hesitated."

"It's confusing." I pause, trying to formulate how I feel in words. "It's just, like, emotional hurt. I thought she was going to be nurturing and take care of me."

"Instead, you got used," Lisa says matter-of-factly.

"Yes. She never cut skin or hit me anywhere you wouldn't normally hit someone with a crop, but …"

"What?"

"She got weird. Really weird."

"How so?" Lisa pauses for a moment and then blurts, "Are you sure you're all right, B?"

"I think so. It was just intense." I tell her how, after she chained up my wrists, her whole demeanor changed. She got quiet and didn't speak to me. And that part, the not knowing, was the scariest part of all. I relay what she did to my body. I am shocked as I hear the words come out of my mouth as I relive it.

"Why didn't you use your safeword?" I'm quiet for way too long, and she says, "B? Why didn't you say anything?"

"After a while, I wanted to. I thought she was treating me like a slave, thinking that's the kind of experience I wanted. It was kind of thrilling at first if I'm honest."

"Thrilling because you still trusted her at that point."

"Yes, exactly. And ... "

"And what, B?"

"I didn't want her to think I was soft or unworthy. I mean, I had no idea she would keep going on and on. When she called me a whore for the first time, that's when I should have spoken up. God, I hate that I am so submissive and reticent that I can't stick up for myself." Tears choke me up, and I can't speak for a moment.

"You're right. She was a wolf in sheep's clothing," she quotes quietly. "A monster mama. I should have stopped you from going."

"Oh, no, no, no, Lisa," I say, rushing past my anguish. "This is in no way your fault. I probably would have gone anyway. But I don't think it would have mattered how long I waited to meet her; the result would have been the same." I sigh and add, "There were parts of the weekend that were good. Parts that I want in my life."

"From her?"

"Oh, God, no." I scoff and then say, "I hope to find someone who will look out for my physical well-being like she was trying to do with the healthy food, exercise, and water. Someone who will show me new experiences."

"Be careful what you wish for," she interjects. "Because it sounds like you got a whole lot of new experiences."

"Humph," I grunt and then tell her about the museum trip and the paintings and other art I saw. "I also want someone who will push my boundaries, but in a safe, trusting way."

"You didn't feel safe?"

"At first, yes. Toward the end? Not so much. You know she didn't even try to stop me from leaving. It was as if she expected me to bolt at that point."

"I'm so relieved you got out of there safely," Lisa said. "When you missed your noon safe call, I figured you'd just lost track of time. But then I started to worry. If you didn't check in by six o'clock, I was going to call the hotel management and have them knock on your door."

"You were?"

"Yes, but …"

"What?"

"I should have done it sooner, B. Waiting might have gotten you hurt." I hear the emotion in her voice, and I choke up again, too. "Or worse."

"I'm sorry I worried you, Lisa. I'm never going to do this again. It's way too risky."

"Famous last words, B," she says.

"I know."

"Listen, drive carefully, and call me when you get home, okay? On another day, we'll talk about how you can go on dates more safely. I wish I lived closer to you."

"Yeah, me, too." We fall into an awkward silence. "Someday, I'll come to visit."

"Same."

"I think I need to find some local friends," I say.

"Don't try to fix it all now, B. Go home. Shower. Eat. Sleep. Call me when you get home. Call me anytime, actually, even if it's two in the morning."

"Thanks, Lisa."

We say our goodbyes, and I am energized enough to drive the rest of the way home. The very first thing I'm going to do when I get home is take a shower and scrub her off every inch of my body.

Chapter 18
One of Us

I barely sleep that first night home from Marquestown. I mean, I am exhausted, but I keep jerking awake with a pounding heart and surging adrenaline. That flight or fight setting is still on active alert, apparently. I must have slept a little, probably from pure exhaustion, because when I wake, it's already light out. I am sore in all kinds of places, especially my shoulders from being shackled to the bedposts for so long. My wrists and ankles have open wounds and rub marks from the cuffs. Oh, and my jaw still hurts from the gags and probably from servicing her so many times. And let's not forget the smothering. Despite the pain, I move my jaw around, and it pops, but in a good way.

Before coffee, I dress and head to a convenience store first thing. I'm not quite awake, but I stock up on the best foods this store has - donuts, cupcakes, cheese puffs, cokes, and frozen pizzas. It's my way of sticking it to the woman who was supposed to nurture me and take care of me.

When I get back to my apartment, I realize that a brand-new year has started. Yep, it's a time to refresh, renew, and start the hell over. Unfortunately, I'm not off to a good start. I don't think I'll ever be able to go to Marquestown ever again without losing my shit. And on top of that, the mail brought me bad news. By some miracle, Jen managed to send me January's rent check on time. Dammit, I'll never get her out of there before her year's lease is up at the end of May. Thank God it's only a year's lease.

I put the bags on the kitchen table and open the freezer door to put the pizzas away. My nipples harden instantly from the cold, and not in a good way. Oh, my God, that hurts. I rub my hands over my shirt and get my nips to settle back down. Coffee, I need coffee. I put the pot on to brew, put the rest of my purchases away, and then sit down at the table with a two-pack of cupcakes. As soon as my butt hits the hard chair, my private parts and my ass remind me how sore I am down there. Both of my holes have been randomly pulsing on their own all morning as if getting ready to orgasm. It's not an unpleasant thing, but it's disconcerting and weird. The nerve endings there are obviously frayed and confused. Kind of like the rest of me. Ha, that'll be the title of my memoir, "Frayed and Confused."

After forever, the coffee is ready, and I drown it with real half-and-half, the way coffee is supposed to be. I sigh and decide that Mama_Luvs never really had my best interest at heart. She was a sadist looking for her next victim to torture for her own pleasure. I am a submissive, not a slave. And, although I know I have some masochist in me, I never wanted to be abused. I want to be cherished and valued.

I want a loving partner. Is that too much to ask? I want a dominant partner who will steer the ship, guide me, and take care of me, too. Sex is *not* all I want. What was it Lisa called her? Oh, yes. Monster Mama. I scoff. That sums it up. All Monster Mama wanted was sex and power. To her, I'm just a fat, lazy millennial. Apparently, that triggered some kind of hatred in her.

At first, I thought she was smothering me with her version of kindness. Now I realize it wasn't kindness at all. And when all of that wasn't enough, she *literally* smothered me with her body. I close my eyes and thank whatever divine forces got me out of there alive. Tears come, but I blink them back. I will not give her the satisfaction.

I march over to my computer and load up *Kinks* so that I can block her and then tell Lisa immediately. That way, Lisa won't think I am a total dolt. When I click on my profile page, I can't believe my eyes. Mama_Luvs left me a message. Do I read it? I shouldn't. I should just block her and be gone. Curiosity gets the better of me.

> MAMA_LUVS: Baby girl, you are a truly wonderful submissive. We still have a lot of work to do together, though. For instance, you could stand to lose 10-15 pounds, do some strength training (your core was notably weak, dear), and you absolutely need some flexibility work. But to be fair, you did well for your first time. I am, however, a bit upset that you left so abruptly.

Your sudden departure was rude and showed atrocious manners – something that will have to be corrected immediately. I have ideas in that regard. Message me when you get a chance, and don't forget to drink your water. Mama_Luvs out.

"Holy shit!" I say to her message. "You are friggin' delusional." I shake my head and take a screenshot of the message to read to Lisa later and then destroy. I take a deep breath and sit back, physically moving away from the message. Should I reply? What the hell would I say? All the things I should have said while she was abusing me? But then I remember a saying I heard once, maybe from Lisa. You can't reason with crazy.

"Nope, you can't." I reach for my mouse and click the message closed. I right-click her name and hover over the block button. "Is this what you want to do, Bernadette?" I ask myself out loud. "Abso-fucking-lutely!" I answer and smash the button. I push the laptop away.

"Hey," I say with a shaky voice and raise my coffee cup high in the air. "That shit is no longer my circus, no longer my monkey. Fuck you and the rice milk you rode in on."

It must be the sugar in the cupcakes that has made me so wise because I realize with brilliant clarity that whatever it is I thought I could have with Mama_Luvs or Mistress Ciara wasn't anything that could be sustained.

But now I am lonelier than ever.

Before I can go down that self-indulging rabbit hole of depression, my phone rings. My heart leaps into my throat. Is it her? It can't be because I never gave her my phone number. Good on me. That's one thing I did right. I look at the caller ID and instantly relax.

"Hey, Lisa," I say, trying to sound chipper.

"How are you holding up?"

"I did it. I blocked her ass."

"And the rest of her, I hope." Lisa laughs at her own joke.

"All of it," I say. "And, you know what? I realized some things." I take a long swig of coffee.

"Tell me."

"I realized that I like sugary snacks and half-and-half in my coffee."

Lisa bursts out laughing.

I then tell her about the message Mama_Luvs sent and read it to her from my screenshot. She agrees that Mama_Luvs is several cards short of a full deck.

"What else did you realize, B?" This time, her tone is more serious.

"That I'm going about things all wrong. I need to make friends. Here. Where I live. I thought I had some, but not a single one reached out to me after the breakup. I think Jen got to them first and spun some tale of woe or whatever."

"That's tough." She makes a clucking noise of disapproval and then gracefully changes the subject. "So, hey, when do you start up at the college again?"

"In five days," I say glumly. "Next Monday."

"So, you have all that time to regroup. That's good, right? At least go for a walk, B."

I shrug even though I know she can't see me.

"Still there, B?"

"Yeah."

She chuckles. "I know you've been through a lot and need time to process, but maybe you shouldn't be alone. Be social somewhere. Anywhere."

"I'll think about it," I say without conviction.

"Keep me posted," she says.

"Oh, shit, you know what?"

"What?"

"I left my water bottle, toothbrush, and toothpaste in the hotel room. And my hairbrush. Dang it."

She scoffs and adds, "Acceptable losses, yes?"

"Yeah, you're right. It just makes me mad. *She* makes me mad."

"Good! She's an asshole, B. I don't know how, but somehow we have to keep you away from the assholes."

"No kidding." We talk for a bit more and then wrap things up. She makes me promise to call her every day. Easy enough.

~~~

176

The days that follow are filled with an inordinate amount of couch surfing and mindless television. I take no walks. I obstinately stay up later than 10:00. I drink the barest amount of water. I eat no vegetables and no fruit. However, I do eat lots of fast food and alternate sugary snacks with salty snacks in the name of a balanced diet. And hey, if I truly am a fat and lazy millennial, like Mama_Luvs said, then great! I embrace it.

And who knew sixteen consecutive hours of home improvement shows a day could be so riveting? I feel more than ready and completely qualified to tear down walls and create that perfect open-concept feel I've always wanted. Ha ha. Too bad I don't live in my own house. And how cool is it that these shows come on one right after the other? I don't even have to change the channel. I am a sloth, and I accept it.

When I wake up Saturday morning, the third day of my sloth existence, my mind is active, and I don't know why. My stomach rejects the notion of donuts for breakfast. Maybe you *can* overload on sugar. Who knew? Instead, I stick to coffee with my usual amount of creamer. Ooh, if I hurry, I can catch the start of the "Flipping Houses Made Easy" marathon. That's the extent of my plans for the day. That and microwaving a frozen box of macaroni and cheese later. Maybe tomorrow, I'll check over my lectures for the spring semester. Probably not. I've been lecturing the same shit for five years now. I can do it in my sleep. Why bother?

I click on the television and hit the couch. Honestly, the urge to dive into the *Kinks* app is powerfully absent from any part of my soul right now. I may go back at some point, but for now, I'm sticking to real life. No more fantasies about the ideal Domme. What is a Domme, anyway? She's a hard-nosed bitch that wants to push around somebody who can't stand up for themselves and won't call out their safeword when they know they should. I smack a fist against my thigh.

"Dammit, you could have at least called yellow, for God's sake. Why the fuck didn't you say something?" I scold myself. "You could have said you weren't cool with what she was doing. You could have told her you were tired of the restraints. But no, you said absolutely nothing." I put my cup down hard on the side table. There are times when beating myself up is close to an Olympic sport, and today, I am going for the gold. "She was probably amazed at how much you let her get away with. She exhausted herself, thinking of new ways to fuck you up. That's why she had no energy to stop you from leaving."

I am so stunned at my words that I can't even tell myself to shut up. I sit in silence while the words echo in my mind. Tears fill my eyes, and I turn off the television. The sobs start shortly after that. I grab two tissues from the box that's migrated to the couch in recent days. Crying jags use up copious amounts of tissues, I've discovered.

"How could I let her do all those things to me?" I say in a tight voice. God, I was so scared toward the end. I trusted a stranger. I didn't know what she was capable of. I'm lucky she let me go. And she knows that, too, doesn't she? She still had all the power in the end. She wins. Fine. Whatever.

I stand up and shuffle to the bathroom for a shower to clear my head. Afterward, I find myself dressing to go out. Rocco's. I'm going to take myself to Rocco's for breakfast. Maybe Marlene will be there. She always makes me feel better, and she doesn't tie me up to the bedposts. I allow myself a small smile.

I tap the pockets of my jeans like I always do. Wallet, phone, and keys. Check. With all present and accounted for, I grab my coat and head out the door and down three flights of stairs. Holy crap, it's snowing. Who knew? My car is covered. I make no move to rethink going out and simply clear off the car.

I sit in a small booth in Marlene's section, and she's there in moments. "Hey, Professor, you're making this some kind of habit, aren't ya?"

Her levity always makes me smile. "Can't stay away, I guess."

She pulls her pad and pen out of her apron. "Don't forget about the breakfast bar. It's your best bet on Saturdays. What can I get you, hun?"

"For now, I'll just have coffee. And a ton of –"

"Creamer," she finishes for me. "I remember. You like a little coffee with your creamer."

"Yeah," I say with a chuckle.

"Coming right up." She tucks the pad and pen back in her apron pocket and hurries away.

For about fifteen minutes, I simply sit in Marlene's section and drink coffee. Sometimes, I people-watch, but mostly, I stare at my coffee. Lisa wouldn't call this socializing, but it's the best I can do at the moment. And just as I think I should go ahead and order food, I hear a familiar voice. I look toward the front door and see her. Oh, shit, this is the first Saturday in the month. The brunch. I can't believe it. My subconscious hoodwinked me into coming here this morning.

"There she is. I told you she would come." Madison waves at me and makes her way over. "Hi, Professor Garneau."

"Hi," I say meekly. Something akin to dread clutches my heart.

"I told them you would come." She gestures back toward three people brushing snow off their coats and taking off scarves and hats. "Please join us, Professor."

"I don't want to intrude," I say. And what I really mean is that I want to go home.

"No, you won't be," she says quickly and takes a step back. "C'mon, c'mon, c'mon. I told them you'd be here. I just knew it." She takes off her wool cap and mittens. Her scarf is bright pink and has a character from that Trolls movie on it. Realization dawns on me. Madison is a *little*. A *little* who just took Calculus. And one of those women standing by the front door is her Mistress.

I find myself getting up without my knowledge. "Okay." My voice sounds a million miles away. I grab my coat, drop a ten on the table for Marlene, and head over to meet Madison's friends.

"Professor," Madison says, "this is my girlfriend, Shasti."

I put out my hand, and we shake. Shasti smiles at me. Her white teeth shine brightly against her dark skin. I think she is of Indian descent, I'm not sure. I estimate that she is a little older than I am, but not by much. Madison also introduces me to the other two women. Rikki's handshake is warm and firm, but Brittany's is cold and limp. It seems that Brittany is Rikki's girlfriend, but I can't be sure. Rikki seems to be about my age, and Brittany in her early twenties, maybe a few years younger than Madison.

"Do you like teaching, Bernadette?" Rikki asks as we're led to the private back room.

Before I can answer, Shasti says, "She's only the best math professor on the planet. Peanut here got an A in her class."

"Impressive," Rikki says to Madison. She turns toward me and says, "Equally impressive."

179

I feel myself blushing to the roots of my hair, and it's not because of the compliment. Rikki has a magnetism to her that I find disarming. Her dark copper-colored hair is pulled back into a ponytail, and it's such an interesting color that I want to reach up and touch it.

I manage not to lose my cool and say, "Madison's a smart cookie. She earned that grade all on her own."

"See, Peanut?" Shasti says to Madison. "Do you believe me now?"

Madison rolls her eyes like a teenager. "I guess."

Everyone except limp-handed Brittany laughs. Maybe she isn't happy about being dragged out in the cold.

The table we sit at is designed for four, so the server places a chair at one end, which I take so I don't break up the couples.

"So, Dr. Garneau," Shasti says, "Madison will be taking Calculus Two this semester. Do you teach that?"

"No, no," I say and order coffee from the server. "I'm still with Calc One."

"Ahh, that's too bad." Shasti purses her lips for a moment and says, "Perhaps we can hire you as Madison's tutor?" She raises her eyebrows expectantly.

I swallow a groan. I hate tutoring. The students always forget to pay, come late, or blame me when they don't pass. "Oh, I uh –"

"Shasti, let her breathe," Rikki says with a laugh.

"You're right, you're right," Shasti says and opens her menu. "Just think about it, okay?"

"Yes, Ma'am," I say and nod in agreement.

An awkward silence follows, and I'm not sure if it has to do with the fact that I basically blew off her request to tutor or if it's something else. Maybe it's because I'm a stranger to everyone except Madison, and they're not sure what to say to me. Oh, God, I should have stayed home. I'm not good in social situations.

We all decide to order the breakfast buffet and stand up to get our food. It isn't long before we're back at the table eating. Thank goodness for the diversion.

"So, uh, how long have you been in the lifestyle?" Brittany asks. There is an underlying *something* in her question. Almost an accusation. I'm not sure what she's getting at.

Before I can ask her what she means, Rikki says, "Mind your manners, Brittany." The stern look she throws her girlfriend would have withered me to the floor.

"Yes, Ma'am," Brittany says with a sneer.

"Eat your food." Rikki's gaze sends Brittany some kind of warning signal.

"Yes, Ma'am," Brittany says again, but this time there is genuine contrite in her voice.

Another awkward silence follows, and I decide that my food is very interesting, and I keep my attention there. Meanwhile, part of me is alternatingly rejoicing and cringing. Rikki and her girlfriend also seem to be in a Dominant/submissive relationship. Realization dawns on me. Brittany thinks I'm into BDSM. That's what she meant by "lifestyle." How the hell can she tell? I've said and done nothing to give it away. But then realization dawns on me. Shit, I called Shasti, "Ma'am." It's so automatic. And if Brittany figured it out, the rest of them did, too.

"So, uh, Bernadette," Shasti says, "are you in a relationship?"

I burst out laughing and then say, "Sorry," at their perplexed expressions. I wipe my mouth with a napkin to hide my frown. "Just ended. Ended badly."

"Oh, I'm so sorry, Professor," Madison says and lays a consoling hand on my wrist.

I wince and pull my hand back. She managed to touch one of my open wounds from the leather cuff. I cover for it by waving off their sympathy about my breakup. "No, no. It's better this way. She wasn't what I thought she would be. She, uh, ..." I can't finish the sentence because my throat chokes up with tears again, and I have to hide my face in my hands.

"Did she do that to you?" Rikki asks. There is anger in her voice.

I choke back my tears and wipe my eyes. "Do what?" I turn to find the most sympathetic pair of green eyes looking back at me.

"This." She gently nudges up the sleeve of my shirt so that my wrist is showing.

Madison gasps, and Shasti clucks in frustration. Brittany grunts as if to say she told them so.

What I hadn't thought to conceal, what I hadn't thought about much at all, were the rub marks from the leather cuffs that I allowed Monster Mama to put on me.

I nod once.

Rikki sighs and says quietly, "Am I right in assuming there are matching marks on the other wrist?"

I nod again.

"And possibly your ankles?"

I nod once more and look down, ashamed. I'm ashamed for all kinds of reasons, mostly that I would let someone do that to me and also that Madison had to see it.

Shasti trades seats with Madison and says, "May I?"

I nod.

Shasti picks up my wrist and examines it. "Leather cuffs?" she asks. There is no judgment in her voice.

"Yes, Ma'am," I say.

"Too tight and left on too long," Rikki says. It's not a question. The anger in her voice is obvious, and I cringe from it.

"Yes," Shasti agrees. "These skin abrasions look fairly clean, but I want you to wash all of them gently using warm water and mild soap. Then petroleum jelly to keep it moist." She turns my wrist over and says, "I recommend some gauze wraps until a scab has started. Then it's best to leave it uncovered." She leans in closer. "This spot right here is worrisome." She takes a quick look at my other wrist and then looks up at me. "This side looks fine. Make sure to check your ankles, though, and you may want to consult your primary doctor."

"Thank you, Ma'am. I'll think about that." Yeah, no. There's no way in hell I'll show these obvious BDSM wounds to my doctor or anyone else.

"The person you just broke up with did this to you?" Rikki asks gently.

"Yes, the visit didn't quite go as I thought it would," I admitted. "I ... She ..." I can't finish. I just met these people, and my job is already in jeopardy. At the moment, I can always deny having said or admitted anything.

"It's okay, dear," Shasti said. "You don't have to tell us anymore."

"I have one question, though," Rikki said. "Was it someone local? Because if it is, I'm going to kick some serious ass."

"No, no, no," I say. "She lives in New York."

"Okay." Rikki blew out an angry breath. "But if this bitch ever crosses my path, she will regret it." A murmur of agreement follows her statement. "Do you want to press charges?"

My eyes grow wide. I hadn't even thought about that. "I-I don't think so."

"You don't have to decide today," Rikki says. Her expression softens, and I feel myself blush from her gaze.

"I have a question, too," Shasti says. "Are you okay? Do you need us to, I don't know, help you in some way?"

"Thank you," I push my sleeves back down over my cuff wounds. "I'll be okay." I turn back to Rikki. "It was just something that got out of hand, but I was able to get out of there and home safe."

"If you're sure," Rikki says softly.

"I think so."

"Well, how about this?" Shasti says. "Call any of us anytime if you need help." She reaches into a pocket and hands me a business card from her wallet. Holy shit, she's an M.D.

"Thank you, Shasti. I appreciate that." My nod of gratitude includes Madison, too.

I turn to thank Rikki and see that she is also holding out a business card. "Oh, cool," I say. "You work at a coffee shop?"

"She *owns* it," Brittany says as if she's talking to a moron.

"Impressive," I say to Rikki, ignoring Brittany, who I realize now is one of those classic brat personalities. I have no idea how anyone, especially someone as nice as Rikki, would be able to put up with her.

I turn to Shasti and send her a pleading look, trying to figure out how to articulate what I want to ask of her and all of them.

"You're safe with us, Bernadette," Shasti says softly. "We're all in the same boat. Our, uh, lifestyle choices make us all vulnerable, but everyone here will honor you as one of us."

"She *is* one of us," Madison says and reaches across the table to pat my hand.

"Absolutely," Brittany says. "Our community is tight-knit, Professor. Please don't worry."

I smile at her and nod my thanks. It's the first serious and grown-up thing she's done in the twenty minutes I've known her.

"No one will find out," Madison says. "And think of it this way, you've made four more friends."

"Perfect," I say, my voice breaking up at the kinship they show me. "Thank you. I've been through …" I pause to take a deep breath, "I've been through a lot this week. Questioning everything." I blow out a sigh and add, "I would love to count you all as friends." I smile at each of them, including Brittany, and this time, my tears are of joy and belonging.

~~~ The End ~~~

Newsletter Signup

Sign up for Danielle Grainger's newsletter to stay on top of new releases. She also likes to provide recommendations for books to read (other than her own, of course).

Sign Up Here:

https://mailchi.mp/32c278368547/danielle-grainger-newsletter

Reviews

Reviews help get my books into the hands of readers who enjoy books like mine. It's often difficult for readers of certain, err, tastes to find books they enjoy. Would you consider writing a review? Let's get the word out. Thank you for at least thinking about it.

About the Author
Danielle Grainger

Dani is an instructor who currently resides in the southeastern USA and has several pampered fur babies. She has always been an avid reader and ventured into writing after reading several novels she felt didn't accurately represent the BDSM lifestyle. With so many rampant misconceptions, she took a chance and crafted admittedly idealized versions of possible experiences. Dani hopes not only to entertain her readers but to enlighten and educate them as well.

Dani's Amazon Author Page:
www.amazon.com/stores/Danielle-Grainger

Dani's Facebook:
facebook.com/danielle.grainger.7777

Dani's Instagram:
DaniGrainger84

Dani's Goodreads Page:
www.goodreads.com/author/show/19699760.Danielle_Grainger

Books by Danielle Grainger

THE DENTON HEIGHTS SERIES

The Denton Heights Series is the series that comes BEFORE the Bernadette Series. This group of books tells the stories of the beloved characters who populate the Bernadette Series world and live the BDSM lifestyle. We learn more about the origin stories of Madison and Shasti; Jaleesa, Tina, Harriet, Dana, DeShawn, and Kari; Rowena and Minjung; and Rikki. Victoria (AKA Daddy Vic), Lydia, and Brittany also feature in this series. The Denton Heights Series is basically the "Prequel Series" to the Bernadette Series.

Under Her Wing (Denton Heights Book 1)
(The Shasti and Madison Story)
An MD/lg age-gap lesbian erotic romance with consensual light BDSM

*** 2023 Finalist in the Golden Crown Literary Society Awards ***

Madison Kim finds herself on a bus headed to Denton Heights, Ohio, a suburb of Cincinnati. Madison is twenty-two-and-three-quarters years old and has a high school diploma, but she isn't smart enough to go to college…so they tell her. Now, she spends her time caring for Mrs. Park, going to the beloved Cincinnati Zoo, and watching movies on her outdated phone. She's not really sure why she's there, but she's taking it day by day. Then, she meets strong, nurturing Miss Shasti at a tea dance.
Shasti Balakrishnan has been looking for someone to call hers for more years than she cares to count. She wants a woman to love and care for in a nurturing Mommy Domme/*little* girl scenario. She's thirty-two and already a partner in a thriving medical clinic in Denton Heights, but truth be told – she's lonely. She thought she'd found a companion in Amber back in D.C., but that fizzled out once they realized they weren't what each other wanted—or needed. And then she meets adorably precocious Madison at a tea dance.

ISBN: 978-1-953734-10-5 (e-Book)
ISBN: 978-1-953734-13-6 (Paperback)

In Her Cage (Denton Heights Book 2)
(The Jaleesa and Tina Story)
A lesbian interracial erotic romance with consensual light BDSM aspects.

Jaleesa Whitmore is a lesbian Domme in and out of fast relationships fueled by sex. She didn't understand addiction. Not yet, anyway. Although she had almost one full year sober, she was done with it. She was moments from heading down the familiar road of drinking that always made her feel good and filled that void. She was about to get her life back on its old track when a fateful encounter with a stranger, who would become a trusted friend, halted her downslide. She didn't know it then, but this encounter would not only lead her to a series of events and people that would change how she looked at life but how she approached it.

Tina Jenkins likes women but is asexual and afraid to try for another relationship. She does understand addiction. Just shy of eleven years clean of her opioid addiction following a dental procedure right out of high school, her parents carefully constructed and monitored everything in her world. It didn't matter that she was thirty-one years old and still living in the pink bedroom in her parents' house. It didn't matter that her mother now had to work from home, and her parents had to track her location and do routine searches of her bag, car, computer, phone, and room. None of it mattered because she was clean.

And then asexual Tina meets promiscuous Jaleesa. And everything changed for both of them.
ISBN: 978-1-953734-28-0 (e-Book)
ISBN: 978-1-953734-29-7 (Paperback)

Within Her Grasp (Denton Heights Book 3)

(The Marta and Shanice Story)
A lesbian age gap interracial erotic romance with consensual light BDSM aspects.

"Within Her Grasp" is an age-gap interracial lesbian romance that tells the tale of two women who had settled for unhappy lives. And then they meet.

White, thirty-something Marta Ingersoll was done with people. She just wanted to be left alone at work and at home, thank you. Her inside cat and the outside stray were all she needed. And her sister, Nora, too, of course. But that was it. And then, one fateful afternoon, her instincts to save a woman in obvious distress kicked in, and her life was shoved onto a strange new course.

Black, twenty-something Shanice Ward never got a break. Life had thrown challenge after challenge at the young woman, and this latest thing was too much, but it wouldn't stop. Woken up from a sound sleep by someone trying to remove her clothing, she shrieked for him to leave her alone. He didn't, but then, the most amazing thing happened. She discovered that superheroes were real, and one had just flown into her room to save her, and her life was shoved onto a strange new course.

ISBN: 978-1-953734-30-3 (e-Book)
ISBN: 978-1-953734-31-0 (Paperback)

By Her Command (Denton Heights Book 4)
(The Rowena and Minjung Story)
A lesbian interracial erotic romance with consensual BDSM aspects.

"By Her Command" is an erotic interracial lesbian romance containing consensual aspects of BDSM. It finds Rowena Tate in need of a submissive who can also manage her household. It's also the tale of Minjung Lee, who is desperate to find a Domme so she won't find herself homeless again. Trust does not come easily for either of them.

Rowena is a white Domme in her late thirties. Through experience, she has come to believe that most, if not all, submissives are selfish creatures who only want what she can provide without considering the person behind the flogger and the paycheck.

Minjung is an East Asian submissive in her mid-thirties. Through experience, she has come to believe that most, if not all, Dominants are selfish creatures who go well beyond contracted limits because there is no one to tell them not to.

Despite their reservations, both are told by members of the Denton Heights BDSM community that they are a good match and lucky to have found each other. Rowena isn't so sure. Neither is Minjung. Time will tell, won't it?

ISBN: 978-1-953734-32-7 (e-Book)
ISBN: 978-1-953734-33-4 (Paperback)

Toward Her Passion (Denton Heights Book 5)
(A Rikki Carmichael Story)
A lesbian erotic reminiscence with consensual BDSM aspects

Rikki Carmichael is strong, stoic, and in charge. She does *not* need help from anyone. She can navigate her own life, thank you very much, and resents her friends' efforts to give her charity. She doesn't take charity; she gives it. Financial troubles threaten to topple her coffee shop business, her livelihood, and her sense of self-worth. Abruptly single and oddly uninterested in finding a new relationship, be it a long-term life partner or a short-term lover, she finds herself reminiscing about past loves and relationships: Hard Eileen, fun Emily, newbie Sarah, and young Jessica.

The anniversary of her mother's death all those years ago sends her into another bout of 'deep downs,' the code words her mother used for Rikki's bouts with depression growing up. Her bestie, Shasti, advises her to make room for someone, a new lover, or a life partner. Shasti wants Rikki to send a message to the universe that she is ready to receive someone into her life. And, lo and behold, in walks Esme, a blonde bombshell customer at the coffee shop. Rikki's hopes are lifted...until they aren't. With no biological family left to lean on, Rikki has to find the strength to become vulnerable and ask for help. Easier said than done. It's much easier to counsel others than to ask for help for herself. She discovers, however, that asking for help is where real strength lies.

ISBN: 978-1-953734-40-2 (e-Book)
ISBN: 978-1-953734-41-9 (Paperback

THE BERNADETTE SERIES

Dr. Bernadette Garneau holds a Ph.D. in Mathematics and has just gotten out of a four-year relationship. Shortly after the breakup, she began an exploration of her repressed sexual desires. One message from a beautiful and powerful online Mistress and Bernadette leaps into the world of BDSM. The Mistress takes charge, and Bernadette reels in the heady power this stranger has over her. She has gotten a taste of the life, and she wants more. She needs more. Several online and in-person experiences with BDSM and Power Exchange have led to cravings she doesn't quite understand. A brief sexual exchange with an online Goddess unleashes an incredible pain-to-pleasure connection that she hadn't understood before. As she sifts through the posers and one-night stands, she homes in on what her submissive nature needs from a Domme. The Bernadette Series follows Bernadette's journey into the world of BDSM and her search for love and sexual satisfaction. As she said, "I want a monogamous partner who wants to not only love and nurture me but who also wants to drape me over her lovely couch and have her way with me."

Wrecking Bernadette
(Book One in the Bernadette Series)
A lesbian's exploration of her sexuality with consensual aspects of BDSM.

Dr. Bernadette Garneau holds a Ph.D. in Mathematics and has been out of a four-year relationship for four months. One good thing about breaking up is that Bernadette is free to explore her repressed sexual desires. One message from a beautiful and powerful online Mistress, and Bernadette leaps into the world of BDSM. Mistress Ciara takes charge, and Bernadette reels in the heady power this stranger has over her. She has gotten a taste of the *life*, and she wants more. She *needs* more.

ISBN: 978-1-953734-00-6 (e-Book)
ISBN: 978-1-953734-14-3 (Paperback)

(S)mothering Bernadette
(Book Two in the Bernadette Series)
A lesbian's continuing exploration of her sexuality with aspects of BDSM.

Dr. Bernadette Garneau's universe is pushing her toward change. Her initial experiences with BDSM and Power Exchange have led to cravings she doesn't quite understand. A brief sexual exchange with an online Goddess unleashes an incredible pain-to-pleasure connection she hadn't understood until that encounter. But after sleeping on it, she clearly understands that this Goddess would never be the long-term relationship she sought.

Disappointed, she wonders if she should just give up and move back to California to be closer to her family. That is until she meets Mama_Luvs, an online Mommy Domme. The woman is nurturing yet stern from the start and is just … perfect. And then Mama_Luvs wants to meet. Starry-eyed Bernadette packs for a New Year's Eve weekend, hoping that this time she's found *the one* – the one who wants to love and nurture her but who also wants to drape her over a couch and have her way with her.

ISBN: 978-1-953734-01-3 (e-Book)
ISBN: 978-1-953734-15-0 (Paperback)

Becoming Bernadette
(Book Three in the Bernadette Series)
A lesbian erotic romance with light consensual BDSM aspects.

University professor Dr. Bernadette Garneau has fallen in love with the world of BDSM. She has a nascent interest in the pain-to-pleasure connection, but she has yet to find partners interested in nurturing the soul within her body that they play with. Admittedly, she's had incredible sexual encounters with experienced Dommes, but all of them left her feeling cold for whatever reason. Most of them simply wanted a sadistic roll in the hay. Bernadette wants a strong Domme who will love and nurture her before flogging her on a St. Andrew's cross and afterward when her body is spent.

One afternoon, she finally musters the courage to venture out and meet some new friends in the local BDSM community. In walks a tall, handsome butch woman with fantastic hair and a confident stride. When this woman asks Bernadette, "Are you collared," Bernadette truthfully answers, "No," and accepts a dinner invitation for that very evening. She is walking on stars when she gets home at 2 a.m. after an ethereal sexual liaison. On the one hand, she wonders who she is becoming – she's never been this promiscuous. And on the other hand, she wonders if this strong butch woman could finally be the Domme of her dreams.

ISBN: 978-1-953734-02-0 (e-Book)
ISBN: 978-1-953734-12-9 (Paperback)

Desiring Bernadette
(Book Four in the Bernadette Series)
A lesbian erotic romance with light consensual BDSM aspects.

*** 2022 Finalist in the Golden Crown Literary Society Awards ***

Rikki Carmichael finally feels that deep D/s relationship she has been craving since her Aunt Tilda introduced her to *the life*. She embraced her dominant side early on, but finding a suitable submissive woman who wanted more than a quick roll in the dungeon proved elusive. That is until Professor Bernadette Garneau arrived on the scene. Now collared and committed to Rikki, will Bernadette prove to be different, or will she turn out like all the others — fickle and full of lies and deception?

And will this perfect sub stay with her when she realizes Rikki's ship is sinking? She'd almost lost the coffee shop she owns when creditors came knocking down her door en masse, seeking payment for debts that weren't hers. Rikki managed to keep her staff and most of her friends in the dark about it, but she has not been able to get out from under it. With high stakes all around, Rikki looks for the peace she is seeking within her relationship with Bernadette. If this one fails, it may be time to leave the life entirely and go live in a cabin somewhere isolated in the woods. But buying a cabin takes money – money she just doesn't have.

ISBN: 978-1-953734-03-7 (e-Book)
ISBN: 978-1-953734-09-9 (Paperback)

Loving Bernadette
(Book Five in the Bernadette Series)
A lesbian erotic romance with light consensual BDSM aspects.

Bernadette Garneau, a beloved professor of mathematics, is a natural submissive. She likes structure and rules and finally found a way of life and a woman who would provide those things for her. The BDSM community she stumbled upon in Denton Heights, Ohio, is where she found Rikki Carmichael, now her dominant partner and fiancée. Rikki is everything she's dreamed of. Yes, Bernadette found the captain of her ship. With Rikki's support and guidance, maybe other parts of her life can finally come together, too – like the respect she deserves but hasn't gotten at the university. Why won't anyone see that she deserves to teach those upper-level courses? And to move out of her closet of an office? What do they know that she does not?

Rikki Carmichael, the respected owner of Rikki's Coffee Shop in town, has finally found the woman of her dreams in super-smart and super-real Bernadette Garneau. Bernadette is a submissive who instinctively knows how to take care of Rikki and accepts Rikki's need to be in charge. Bernadette is the first submissive Rikki's ever had that wasn't solely out for her own gain. Once Rikki can climb out of the deep financial debt she's found herself in, she will finally make their engagement to be married public.

Miscommunication, faulty assumptions, and unmet expectations threaten this union seemingly made in heaven. When life comes at them hard and fast, they must rely on their bond and their loving, self-made family of friends.

ISBN: 978-1-953734-08-2 (e-Book)
ISBN: 978-1-953734-11-2 (Paperback)

www.ingramcontent.com/pod-product-compliance
Lightning Source LLC
Chambersburg PA
CBHW071201260626
47162CB00003B/1134